Every one who could walk, creep, or fly headed
for the Old Briar-patch.

CHILDREN'S THRIFT CLASSICS

Mrs. Peter Rabbit

THORNTON W. BURGESS

Original Illustrations
Adapted by Thea Kliros

PUBLISHED IN ASSOCIATION WITH THE
THORNTON W. BURGESS MUSEUM AND THE
GREEN BRIAR NATURE CENTER, SANDWICH, MASSACHUSETTS
BY
DOVER PUBLICATIONS, INC., MINEOLA, NEW YORK

DOVER CHILDREN'S THRIFT CLASSICS

GENERAL EDITOR: STANLEY APPELBAUM
EDITOR OF THIS VOLUME: STEVEN PALMÉ

Copyright

Bibliographical Note

This Dover edition, first published in 1996 in association with the Thornton W. Burgess Museum and the Green Briar Nature Center, Sandwich, Massachusetts, who have provided a new introduction, is an unabridged republication of the work first published by Little, Brown, and Company, Boston, in 1919. The original illustrations by Harrison Cady have been adapted for this new edition by Thea Kliros.

Library of Congress Cataloging-in-Publication Data

Burgess, Thornton W. (Thornton Waldo), 1874–1965.
    Mrs. Peter Rabbit / Thornton W. Burgess ; original illustrations adapted by Thea Kliros.
        p.   cm. — (Dover children's thrift classics)
    "Published in association with the Thornton W. Burgess Museum and the Green Briar Nature Center, Sandwich, Massachusetts."
    Summary: When Peter Rabbit convinces Little Miss Fuzzy Tail to marry him and come to live in the Dear Old Briar Patch, he finds true happiness and learns responsibility.
    ISBN 0-486-29376-9 (pbk.)
    [1. Rabbits—Fiction. 2. Animals—Fiction.] I. Kliros, Thea, ill. II. Title. III. Series.
PZ7.B917Mr   1996
[E]—dc20   96-21745
                                             CIP
                                             AC

Manufactured in the United States of America
Dover Publications, Inc., 31 East 2nd Street, Mineola, N.Y. 11501

Introduction to *Mrs. Peter Rabbit*

PETER RABBIT was restless and lonesome. Since Peter is always looking for a good adventure, he decided it was time to explore the Great World and visit the Green Pasture. Peter had always heard Sammy Jay say what a wonderful place it was and he was anxious to see for himself. While in the Green Pasture, Peter encountered two of the softest, gentlest eyes he had ever seen peeping up at him from behind a fern. It was Little Miss Fuzzytail! Peter Rabbit began to fall in love. By reading the story, you will learn how Peter convinces Little Miss Fuzzytail to become Mrs. Peter Rabbit and live with him in the Dear Old Briar Patch. Peter must also outwit Old Man Coyote and Hooty the Owl on the journey home. In this story, Peter Rabbit finds true happiness and learns responsibility. At the end of the tale, Mrs. Peter has a big secret to tell all the little forest folks.

Mrs. Peter Rabbit was originally published in 1919. This story is one of the 170 books written by Thornton W. Burgess, children's author and naturalist. Mr. Burgess was born in Sandwich, Massachusetts, on Cape Cod, in 1874. As a boy, he spend time exploring the fields, salt marshes and forests of Sandwich—experiences which fostered a lifelong love of nature and wildlife. He passed on this love through the magic tales he wrote for his own son and later published for all the children of the world to enjoy.

For the past twenty years, the Thornton W. Burgess Society, a non-profit organization in Sandwich, has continued to educate children and adults about the natural world. The Society operates the Thornton W. Burgess Museum, which honor the life and work of this extraordinary man and the Green Briar Nature Center, which carries out his goals of preservation and environmental education.

Contents

List of Illustrations

I

Peter Rabbit Loses His Appetite

Good appetite, you'll always find,
Depends upon your state of mind.
Peter Rabbit

PETER RABBIT HAD lost his appetite. Now when Peter Rabbit loses his appetite, something is very wrong indeed with him. Peter has boasted that he can eat any time and all the time. In fact, the two things that Peter thinks most about are his stomach and satisfying his curiosity, and nearly all of the scrapes that Peter has gotten into have been because of those two things. So when Peter loses his appetite or his curiosity, there is surely something the matter with him.

Ever since Old Man Coyote had come to live on the Green Meadows, Peter had been afraid to go very far from the dear Old Briar-patch where he makes his home, and where he always feels safe. Now there wasn't any reason why he should go far from the dear Old Briar-patch. There was plenty to eat in it and all around it, for sweet clover grew almost up to the very edge of it, and you know Peter is very fond of sweet clover. So there was plenty for Peter to eat without running any risk of danger. With nothing to do but eat and sleep, Peter should have grown fat and contented. But he didn't.

1

Now that is just the way with a lot of people. The more they have and the less they have to worry about, the more discontented they become, and at last they are positively unhappy. There was little Danny Meadow Mouse, living out on the Green Meadows; he was happy all the livelong day, and yet he had no safe castle like the dear Old Briar-patch where he could always be safe. Every minute of every day Danny had to keep his eyes wide open and his wits working their very quickest, for any minute he was likely to be in danger. Old Man Coyote or Reddy Fox or Granny Fox or Digger the Badger or Mr. Blacksnake was likely to come creeping through the grass any time, and they are always hungry for a fat Meadow Mouse. And as if that weren't worry enough, Danny had to watch the sky, too, for Old Whitetail the Marsh Hawk, or his cousin Redtail, or Blacky the Crow, each of whom would be glad of a Meadow Mouse dinner. Yet in spite of all this, Danny was happy and never once lost his appetite.

But Peter Rabbit, with nothing to worry him so long as he stayed in the Old Briar-patch, couldn't eat and grew more and more unhappy.

"I don't know what's the matter with me. I really don't know what's the matter with me," said Peter, as he turned up his nose at a patch of sweet, tender young clover. "I think I'll go and cut some new paths through the Old Briar-patch."

Now, though he didn't know it, that was the very best thing he could do. It gave him something to think about. For two or three days he was very busy cutting new paths, and his appetite came back. But when he had made all the paths he wanted, and there was nothing else to do, he lost his appetite again. He just sat still all day long and moped and thought and thought and thought. The trouble with Peter Rabbit's thinking was that it was all about himself and how unhappy he was. Of course,

"I believe I'm just lonesome," said Peter.

the more he thought about this, the more unhappy he grew.

"If I only had some one to talk to, I'd feel better," said he to himself. That reminded him of Johnny Chuck and what good times they used to have together when Johnny lived on the Green Meadows. Then he thought of how happy Johnny seemed with his family in his new home in the Old Orchard, in spite of all the worries his family made him. And right then Peter found out what was the matter with him.

"I believe I'm just lonesome," said Peter. "Yes, Sir, that's what's the matter with me.

> "It isn't good to be alone,
>   I've often heard my mother say.
> It makes one selfish, grouchy, cross,
>   And quite unhappy all the day.
> One needs to think of other folks,
>   And not of just one's self alone,
> To find the truest happiness,
>   And joy and real content to own.

"Now that I've found out what is the trouble with me, the question is, what am I going to do about it?"

II

Peter Rabbit Plans a Journey

It's a long jump that makes no landing.
Peter Rabbit

"THE TROUBLE WITH me is that I'm lonesome," repeated Peter Rabbit as he sat in the dear Old Briar-patch. "Yes, Sir, that's the only thing that's wrong with me. I'm just tired of myself, and that's why I've lost my appetite. And now I know what's the matter, what am I going to do about it? If I were sure, absolutely sure, that Old Man Coyote meant what he said about our being friends, I'd start out this very minute to call on all my old friends. My, my, my, it seems an age since I visited the Smiling Pool and saw Grandfather Frog and Jerry Muskrat and Billy Mink and Little Joe Otter! Mr. Coyote sounded as if he really meant to leave me alone, but, but—well, perhaps he did mean it when he saw me sitting here safe among the brambles, but if I should meet him out in the open, he might change his mind and—oh, dear, his teeth are terrible long and sharp!"

Peter sat a little longer, thinking and thinking. Then a bright idea popped into his head. He kicked up his heels.

"I'll do it," said he. "I'll make a journey! That's what I'll do! I'll make a journey and see the Great World.

"By staying here and sitting still
I'm sure I'll simply grow quite ill.
A change of scene is what I need
To be from all my trouble freed."

Of course if Peter had really stopped to think the matter over thoroughly he would have known that running away from one kind of trouble is almost sure to lead to other troubles. But Peter is one of those who does his thinking afterward. Peter is what is called impulsive. That is, he does things and then thinks about them later, and often wishes he hadn't done them. So now the minute the idea of making a journey popped into his head, he made up his mind that he would do it, and that was all there was to it. You see, Peter never looks ahead. If he could get rid of the trouble that bothered him now, which, you know, was nothing but lonesomeness, he wouldn't worry about the troubles he might get into later.

Now the minute Peter made up his mind to make a journey, he began to feel better. His lost appetite returned, and the first thing he did was to eat a good meal of sweet clover.

"Let me see," said he, as he filled his big stomach, "I believe I'll visit the Old Pasture. It's a long way off and I've never been there, but I've heard Sammy Jay say that it's a very wonderful place, and I don't believe it is any more dangerous than the Green Meadows and the Green Forest, now that Old Man Coyote and Reddy and Granny Fox are all living here. I'll start to-night when I am sure that Old Man Coyote is nowhere around, and I won't tell a soul where I am going."

So Peter settled himself and tried to sleep the long day away, but his mind was so full of the long journey he was going to make that he couldn't sleep much, and when he did have a nap, he dreamed of wonderful sights and adventures out in the Great World. At last he saw jolly, round, red Mr. Sun drop down to his bed behind the Purple Hills. Old Mother West Wind came hurrying back from her day's work and gathered her children, the Merry Little Breezes, into her big bag, and then she, too, started for her home behind the Purple Hills. A little star came out and winked at Peter, and then way over on the edge of the Green Forest he heard Old Man Coyote laugh. Peter grinned. That was what he had been waiting for, since it meant that Old Man Coyote was so far away that there was nothing to fear from him.

Peter hopped out from the dear, safe Old Briar-patch, looked this way and that way, and then, with his heart in his mouth, started towards the Old Pasture as fast as he could go, lipperty—lipperty—lip.

III

Hooty the Owl Changes His Hunting Grounds

A full stomach makes a pleasant day;
An empty stomach turns the whole word gray.
Peter Rabbit

HOOTY THE OWL sat on the tip-top of a tall dead tree in the Green Forest while the Black Shadows crept swiftly among the trees. He was talking to himself. It wouldn't have done for him to have spoken aloud what he was saying to himself, for then the little people in feathers and fur on whom he likes to make his dinner would have heard him and known just where he was. So he said it to himself, and sat so still that he looked for all the world like a part of the tree on which he was sitting. What he was saying was this:

"Towhit, towhoo! Towhit, towhoo!
Will some one tell me what to do?
My children have an appetite
That keeps me hunting all the night,
And though their stomachs I may stuff
They never seem to have enough.
Towhit, towhoo! Towhit, towhoo!
Will some one tell me what to do?"

When it was dark enough he gave his fierce hunting call—"Whooo-hoo-hoo, whoo-hoo!"

Now that is a terrible sound in the dark woods, very terrible indeed to the little forest people, because it sounds so fierce and hungry. It makes them jump and shiver, and that is just what Hooty wants them to do, for in doing it one of them is likely to make just the least scratching with his claws, or to rustle a leaf. If he does, Hooty, whose ears are very, very wonderful, is almost sure to hear, and with his great yellow eyes see him, and then—Hooty has his dinner.

The very night when Peter Rabbit started on his journey to the Old Pasture, Hooty the Owl had made up his mind that something had got to be done to get more food for those hungry babies of his up in the big hemlock-tree in the darkest corner of the Green Forest. Hunting was very poor, very poor indeed, and Hooty was at his wits' end to know what he should do. He had hooted and hooted in vain in the Green Forest, and he had sailed back and forth over the Green Meadows like a great black shadow without seeing so much as a single Mouse.

"It's all because of Old Man Coyote and Granny and Reddy Fox," said Hooty angrily. "They've spoiled the hunting. Yes, Sir, that's just what they have done! If I expect to feed those hungry babies of mine, I must find new hunting grounds. I believe I'll go up to the Old Pasture. Perhaps I'll have better luck up there."

So Hooty the Owl spread his broad wings and started for the Old Pasture just a little while after Peter Rabbit had started for the same place. Of course he didn't know that Peter was on his way there, and of course Peter didn't know that Hooty even thought of the Old Pasture. If he had, perhaps he would have thought twice before starting. Anyway, he would have kept a sharper watch on the sky. But as it was his thoughts were all of Old Man Coyote and Granny Fox, and that is where Peter made a very grave mistake, a very grave mistake indeed, as he was soon to find out.

IV

The Shadow with Sharp Claws

> Now what's the use, pray tell me this,
>   When all is said and done;
> A thousand things and one to learn
>   And then forget this one?
> For when that one alone you need,
>   And nothing else will do,
> What good are all the thousand then?
>   I do not see; do you?
>
> *Peter Rabbit*

FORGETTING LEADS TO more trouble than almost any-thing under the sun. Peter Rabbit knew this. Of course he knew it. Peter had had many a narrow escape just from forgetting something. He knew just as well as you know that he might just as well not learn a thing as to learn it and then forget it. But Peter is such a happy-go-lucky little fellow that he is very apt to forget, and forgetting leads him into all kinds of difficulties, just as it does most folks.

Now Peter had learned when he was a very little fellow

that when he went out at night, he must watch out quite as sharply for Hooty the Owl as for either Granny or Reddy Fox, and usually he did. But the night he started to make a journey to the Old Pasture, his mind was so full of Old Man Coyote and Granny and Reddy Fox that he wholly forgot Hooty the Owl. So, as he scampered across the Green Meadows, lipperty—lipperty—lip, as fast as he could go, with his long ears and his big eyes and his wobbly nose all watching out for danger on the ground, not once did he think that there might be danger from the sky above him.

It was a moonlight night, and Peter was sharp enough to keep in the shadows whenever he could. He would scamper as fast as he knew how from one shadow to another and then sit down in the blackest part of each shadow to get his breath, and to look and listen and so make sure that no one was following him. The nearer he got to the Old Pasture, the safer he felt from Old Man Coyote and Granny and Reddy Fox. When he scampered across the patches of moonshine his heart didn't come up in his mouth the way it had at first. He grew bolder and bolder. Once or twice he stopped for a mouthful of sweet clover. He was tired, for he had come a long way, but he was almost to the Old Pasture now, and it looked very dark and safe, for it was covered with bushes and brambles.

"Plenty of hiding places there," thought Peter. "It really looks as safe as the dear Old Briar-patch. No one will ever think to look for me way off here."

Just then he spied a patch of sweet clover out in the moonlight. His mouth began to water. "I'll just fill my stomach before I go into the Old Pasture, for there may not be any clover there," said Peter.

"You'd better be careful, Peter Rabbit," said a wee warning voice inside him.

He dodged and jumped, and all the time the
shadow followed him.

"Pooh!" said Peter. "There's nothing to be afraid of way up here!"

A shadow drifted across the sweet clover patch. Peter saw it. "That must be made by a cloud crossing the moon," said Peter, and he was so sure of it that he didn't even look up to see, but boldly hopped out to fill his stomach. Just as he reached the patch of clover, the shadow drifted over it again. Then all in a flash a terrible thought entered Peter's head. He didn't stop to look up. He suddenly sprang sideways, and even as he did so, sharp claws tore his coat and hurt him dreadfully. He twisted and dodged and jumped and turned this way and that way, and all the time the shadow followed him. Once again sharp claws tore his coat and made him squeal with pain.

At last, when his breath was almost gone, he reached the edge of the Old Pasture and dived under a friendly old bramble-bush.

"Oh," sobbed Peter, "I forgot all about Hooty the Owl! Besides, I didn't suppose he ever came way up here."

V

In the Old Pasture

Brambles never scratch those who understand
and are considerate of them.
Peter Rabbit

PETER RABBIT SAT under a friendly bramble-bush on the edge of the Old Pasture and panted for breath, while his heart went pit-a-pat, pit-a-pat, as if it would thump its way right through his sides. Peter had had a terrible fright. There were long tears in his coat, and he smarted and ached dreadfully where the cruel claws of Hooty the Owl had torn him. And there he was in a strange place, not knowing which way to turn, for you know he never had visited the Old Pasture before.

But Peter had had so many narrow escapes in his life that he had learned not to worry over dangers that are past. Peter is what wise men call a phi-los-o-pher. That is a big word, but its meaning is very simple. A philosopher is one who believes that it is foolish to think about things that have happened, except to learn some lesson from them, and that the best thing to do is to make the most of the present. Peter had learned his lesson. He was sure of that.

"I never, never will forget again to watch out for Hooty the Owl," said he to himself, as he nursed his wounds, "and so perhaps it is a good thing that he so nearly caught me this time. If he hadn't, I might have forgotten all about him some time when he could catch me. I certainly wouldn't have watched out for him way up here, for I didn't think he ever came up to the Old Pasture. But now I know he does, Mr. Hooty'll have to be smarter than he's ever been before to catch me napping again. My, how I do smart and ache! I know now just how Danny Meadow Mouse felt that time Hooty caught him and dropped him into the Old Briar-patch. Ouch! Well, as my mother used to say:

'Yesterday has gone away,
Make the most of just to-day.'

Here I am up in the Old Pasture, and the question is, what shall I do next?"

Peter felt a queer little thrill as he peeped out from under the friendly bramble-bush. Very strange and wonderful it seemed. Of course he couldn't see very far, because the

Old Pasture was all overgrown with bushes and briars, and they made the very blackest of black shadows in the moonlight. Peter wondered what dangers might be awaiting him there, but somehow he didn't feel much afraid. No, Sir, he didn't feel much afraid. You see those briars looked good to him, for briars are always friendly to Peter and unfriendly to those who would do harm to Peter. So when he saw them, he felt almost at home.

Peter drew a long breath. Then he cried "Ouch!" You see, he had forgotten for a minute how sore he was. He was eager to explore this new wonderland, for Sammy Jay had told him wonderful tales about it, and he knew that here old Granny Fox and Reddy Fox had found safety when Farmer Brown's boy had hunted for them so hard on the Green Meadows and in the Green Forest. He felt sure that there must be the most splendid hiding-places, and it seemed as if he certainly must start right out to see them, for you know Peter is very, very curious. But the first move he made brought another "Ouch" from him, and he made up a wry face.

"I guess the best thing for me to do is to stay right where I am," said he, "for here I am safe under this friendly old bramble."

So with a sigh Peter settled down to make himself as comfortable as he could, and once, as far, far away on the Green Meadows he heard the voice of Old Man Coyote, Peter even smiled.

"I haven't anything to fear from him, anyway, for he'll never think of coming way up here," said he.

VI

Peter Rabbit Is Still Lonesome

A sympathetic word or two
A wond'rous help is, when you're blue.
So pity him who sits alone
His aches and troubles to bemoan.

Peter Rabbit

ALL THE REST of that night Peter sat under a friendly old bramble-bush on the edge of the Old Pasture and nursed the sore places made by the claws of Hooty the Owl. At last jolly, round, red Mr. Sun began to climb up in the blue, blue sky, just as he does every day. Peter looked up at him, and he felt sure that Mr. Sun winked at him. Somehow it made him feel better. The fact is, Peter was beginning to feel just a wee, wee bit homesick. It is bad enough to be in a strange place alone, but to be sore and to smart and ache as Peter did makes that lonesome feeling a whole lot harder to bear. It is dreadful not to have any one to speak to, but to look around and not see a single thing you have ever seen before,—my, my, my, it certainly does give you a strange, sinking feeling way down inside!

Before that long night was over Peter felt as if his heart had gone way down to his very toes. Yes, Sir, that's the way he felt. Every time he moved at all he cried "Ouch!" He just knew that he was growing more stiff and sore every minute. Then he began to wonder what he should do for something to eat, for he was in a strange place, you remember. And that made him think of all his private little paths through the dear Old Briar-patch, the little paths he had made all himself, and which no one used but himself, excepting Danny Meadow Mouse when he came for a visit.

"Perhaps I shall never, never see them again," moaned Peter, and two big tears filled his eyes and were just ready to drop.

At that moment he looked up and saw jolly, round, red Mr. Sun wink. Peter tried to wink back, and that made the two tears fall. But there were no more tears to follow. You see that wink had made all the difference in the world. Peter's heart had jumped right back where it belonged. Mr. Sun was one of his oldest friends and you know

> When trouble comes, a friendly face
> Makes bright the very darkest place.

And so, just as he made bright all the Old Pasture, Mr. Sun also made bright the dark little corners in Peter's heart just because he was an old friend. To be sure Peter was still lonesome, but it was a different kind of lonesomeness. He hadn't anybody to talk to, which is always a dreadful thing to Peter, but he had only to look up to catch a friendly wink, and somehow that not only made him feel better inside but it seemed to make his aches and smarts better too.

VII

Peter Finds Tracks

Every day is different from every other day,
And always there is something new to see
along the way.

Peter Rabbit

PETER RABBIT HAD sat still just as long as he could. He
was stiff and lame and sore from the wounds made by
Hooty the Owl, but his curiosity wouldn't let him sit
still a minute longer. He just *had* to explore the Old Pasture. So with many a wry face and many an "Ouch" he
limped out from the shelter of the friendly old bramble-
bush and started out to see what the Old Pasture was like.

Now Hooty the Owl had taught Peter wisdom. With his
torn clothes and his aches and smarts he couldn't very
well forget to be careful. First he made sure that there
was no danger near, and this time he took pains to look
all around in the sky as well as on the ground. Then he
limped out to the very patch of sweet clover where Hooty
had so nearly caught him the night before.

"A good breakfast," said Peter, "will make a new Rabbit
of me." You know Peter thinks a great deal of his stomach.
So he began to eat as fast as he could, stopping every
other mouthful to look and listen. "I know it's a bad habit
to eat fast," said he, "but it's a whole lot worse to have an
empty stomach." So he ate and ate and ate as fast as he
could make his little jaws go, which is very fast indeed.

When Peter's stomach was stuffed full he gave a great
sigh of relief and limped back to the friendly old bramble-
bush to rest. But he couldn't sit still long, for he just had

to find out all about the Old Pasture. So pretty soon he started out to explore. Such a wonderful place as it seemed to Peter! There were clumps of bushes with little open spaces between, just the nicest kind of playgrounds. Then there were funny spreading, prickly juniper-trees, which made the very safest places to crawl out of harm's way and to hide. Everywhere were paths made by cows. Very wonderful they seemed to Peter, who had never seen any like them before. He liked to follow them because they led to all kinds of queer places.

Sometimes he would come to places where tall trees made him think of the Green Forest, only there were never more than a few trees together. Once he found an old tumble-down stone wall all covered with vines, and he shouted right out with delight.

"It's a regular castle!" cried Peter, and he knew that there he would be safe from every one but Shadow the Weasel. But he never was wholly safe from Shadow the Weasel anywhere, so he didn't let that thought worry him. By and by he came to a wet place called a swamp. The ground was soft, and there were little pools of water. Great ferns grew here just as they did along the bank of the Laughing Brook, only more of them. There were pretty birch-trees and wild cherry-trees. It was still and dark and oh, so peaceful! Peter liked that place and sat down under a big fern to rest. He didn't hear a sound excepting the beautiful silvery voice of Veery the Thrush. Listening to it, Peter fell asleep, for he was very tired.

By and by Peter awoke. For a minute he couldn't think where he was. Then he remembered. But for a long time he sat perfectly still, thinking of his adventures and wondering if he would be missed down on the Green Meadows. Then all of a sudden Peter saw something that made him sit up so suddenly that he cried "Ouch!" for he had forgotten all about how stiff and sore he was.

What do you think Peter saw? Tracks! Yes, Sir, he saw tracks, Rabbit tracks in the soft mud, and Peter knew that he hadn't made them!

VIII

The Strange Tracks in the Old Pasture

Who has attentive ear and eye
Will learn a lot if he but try.
                              Peter Rabbit

PETER RABBIT STARED and stared at the tracks in the soft mud of the swamp in the Old Pasture. He would look first at the tracks, then at his own feet, and finally back at the tracks again. He scratched his long right ear with his long right hind foot. Then he scratched his long left ear with his long left hind foot, all the time staring his hardest at those strange tracks. They certainly were the tracks of a Rabbit, and it was equally certain that they were not his own.

"They are too big for mine, and they are too small for Jumper the Hare's. Besides, Jumper is in the Green Forest and not way off up here," said Peter to himself. "I wonder—well, I wonder if he will try to drive me away."

You see Peter knew that if he had found a strange Rabbit in his dear Old Briar-patch he certainly would have tried his best to drive him out, for he felt that the Old Briar-patch belonged to him. Now he wondered if the maker of these tracks would feel the same way about the Old Pasture. Peter looked troubled as he thought it over. Then his face cleared.

Peter stared and stared at the tracks in the soft mud.

"Perhaps," said he hopefully, "he is a new comer here, too, and if he is, I'll have just as much right here as he has. Perhaps he simply has big feet and isn't any bigger or stronger than I am, and if that's the case I'd like to see him drive me out!"

Peter swelled himself out and tried to look as big as he could when he said this, but swelling himself out this way reminded him of how stiff and sore he was from the wounds given him by Hooty the Owl, and he made a wry face. You see he realized all of a sudden that he didn't feel much like fighting.

"My," said Peter, "I guess I'd better find out all about this other fellow before I have any trouble with him. The Old Pasture looks big enough for a lot of Rabbits, and perhaps if I don't bother him, he won't bother me. I wonder what he looks like. I believe I'll follow these tracks and see what I can find."

So Peter began to follow the tracks of the strange Rabbit, and he was so interested that he almost forgot to limp. They led him this way and they led him that way through the swamp and then out of it. At the foot of a certain birch-tree Peter stopped.

"Ha!" said he, "now I shall know just how big this fellow is."

How was he to know? Why, that tree was a kind of Rabbit measuring-stick. Yes, Sir, that is just what it was. You see, Rabbits like to keep a record of how they grow, just as some little boys and girls do, but as they have no doors or walls to stand against, they use trees. And this was the measuring-tree of the Rabbit whose tracks Peter had been following. Peter stopped at the foot of it and sat down to think it over. He knew what the tree meant perfectly well. He had one or two measuring-trees of his own on the edge of the Green Forest. He knew, too, that it was more than a mere measuring-tree. It was a kind of "no trespassing" sign. It meant that some other Rabbit had lived here for some time and felt that he owned this part of the Old Pasture. Peter's nose told him that, for the tree smelled very, very strong of Rabbit—of the Rabbit with the big feet. This was because whoever used it for a measuring-tree used to rub himself against it as far up as he could reach.

Peter hopped up close to it. Then he sat up very straight and stretched himself as tall as he could, but he wisely took care not to rub against the tree. You see, he didn't want to leave his own mark there. So he stretched and stretched, but stretch as he would, he couldn't make his wobbly little nose reach the mark made by the other Rabbit.

"My sakes, he is a big fellow!" exclaimed Peter. "I guess I don't want to meet him until I feel better and stronger than I do now."

IX

An Unpleasant Surprise

Legs are very useful when you want to run
     away;
Long, sharp teeth are splendid if to fight you
     want to stay;
But a far, far greater blessing, whether one
     may stay or quit,
Is a clever, trusty, quick and ever ready wit.

Peter Rabbit

PETER RABBIT SAT in a snug hiding-place in the Old Pasture and thought over what he had found out about the strange Rabbit whose tracks he had followed. They had led him to a rubbing or measuring-tree, where the strange Rabbit had placed his mark, and that mark was so high up on the tree that Peter knew the strange Rabbit must be a great deal bigger than himself.

"If he's bigger, of course he is stronger," thought Peter, "and if he is both bigger and stronger, of course it won't be the least bit of use for me to fight him. Then, anyway, I'm too stiff and sore to fight. And then, he has no business to think he owns the Old Pasture, because he doesn't. I have just as much right here as he has. Yes, Sir, I have just as much right in this Old Pasture as he has, and if he thinks he can drive me out he is going to find that he was never more mistaken in his life! I'll show him! Yes, Sir-e-e, I'll show him! I guess my wits are as sharp as his, and I wouldn't wonder if they are a little bit sharper."

Foolish Peter Rabbit! There he was boasting and bragging to himself of what he would do to some one whom he hadn't even seen, all because he had found a sign that told him the Old Pasture, in which he had made up his mind to make his new home, was already the home of some one else. Peter was like a lot of other people; he wasn't fair. No, Sir, he wasn't fair. He let his own desires destroy his sense of fair play. It was all right for him to put up signs in the dear Old Briar-patch and the Green Forest, warning other Rabbits that they must keep away, but it was all wrong for another Rabbit to do the same thing in the Old Pasture. Oh, my, yes! That was quite a different matter! The very thought of it made Peter very, very angry. When he thought of this other Rabbit, it was always as the stranger. That shows just how unfair Peter was, because, you see, Peter himself was really the stranger. It was his first visit to the Old Pasture, while it was very plain that the other had lived there for some time.

But Peter couldn't or wouldn't see that. He had counted

so much on having the Old Pasture to himself and doing as he pleased, that he was too upset and disappointed to be fair. If the other Rabbit had been smaller than he—well, that might have made a difference. The truth is, Peter was just a wee bit afraid. And perhaps it was that wee bit of fear that made him unfair and unjust. Anyway, the longer he sat and thought about it, the angrier he grew, and the more he bragged and boasted to himself about what he would do.

"I'll just keep out of sight until my wounds are healed, and then we'll see who owns the Old Pasture!" thought Peter.

No sooner had this thought popped into his head than he received a surprise, such an unpleasant surprise! It was three heavy thumps right behind him. Peter knew what that meant. Of course he knew. It meant that he must run or fight. It meant that he had been so busy thinking about how smart he was going to be that he had forgotten to cover his own tracks, and so the maker of the big tracks he had followed had found him out.

Thump! Thump! Thump! There it was again. Peter knew by the sound that it was of no use to stay and fight, especially when he was so sore and stiff. There was nothing to do but run away. He simply had to. And that is just what he did do, while his eyes were filled with tears of rage and bitterness.

X

Peter Rabbit Almost Decides to Return Home

*I have no doubt that you've been told
How timid folks are sometimes bold.*
Peter Rabbit

IN ALL HIS life Peter Rabbit had never been so disappointed. Here he was in the Old Pasture, about which he had dreamed and thought so long, and in reaching which he had had such a narrow escape from Hooty the Owl, and yet he was unhappy. The fact is, Peter was more unhappy than he could remember ever to have been before. Not only was he unhappy, but he was in great fear, and the worst of it was he was in fear of an enemy who could go wherever he could go himself.

You see, it was this way: Peter had expected to find some enemies in the Old Pasture. He had felt quite sure that fierce old Mr. Goshawk was to be watched for, and perhaps Mr. Redtail and one or two others of the Hawk family. He knew that Granny and Reddy Fox had lived there once upon a time and might come back if things got too unpleasant for them on the Green Meadows, now that Old Man Coyote had made his home there. But Peter didn't worry about any of these dangers. He was used to them, was Peter. He had been dodging them ever since he could remember. A friendly bramble-bush, a little patch of briars, or an old stone wall near was all that Peter needed to feel perfectly safe from these enemies. But now he was in danger wherever he went, for he had an enemy who could go everywhere he could, and it seemed to Peter that this enemy was following him all the time. Who was it? Why, it was a great big old Rabbit with a very short temper, who, because he had lived there for a long time, felt that he owned the Old Pasture and that Peter had no right there.

Now, in spite of all his trouble, Peter had seen enough of the Old Pasture to think it a very wonderful place, a very wonderful place indeed. He had seen just enough to want to see more. You know how very curious Peter is. It seemed to him that he just couldn't go back to the dear Old Briar-patch on the Green Meadows until he had seen everything to be seen in the Old Pasture. So he couldn't make up his mind to go back home, but stayed and stayed, hoping each day that the old gray Rabbit would get tired of hunting for him, and would let him alone.

But the old gray Rabbit didn't do anything of the kind. He seemed to take the greatest delight in waiting until Peter thought that he had found a corner of the Old Pasture where he would be safe, and then in stealing there when Peter was trying to take a nap, and driving him out. Twice Peter had tried to fight, but the old gray Rabbit was too big for him. He knocked all the wind out of poor Peter with a kick from his big hind legs, and then with his sharp teeth he tore Peter's coat.

Poor Peter! His coat had already been badly torn by the cruel claws of Hooty the Owl, and Old Mother Nature hadn't had time to mend it when he fought with the old gray Rabbit. After the second time Peter didn't try to fight again. He just tried to keep out of the way. And he did, too. But in doing it he lost so much sleep and he had so little to eat that he grew thin and thin and thinner, until, with his torn clothes, he looked like a scarecrow.

> And still he hated to give in
> When there was still so much to see.
> "Persistence, I was taught, will win,
> And so I will persist," said he.

And he did persist day after day, until at last he felt that
he really must give it up. He had stretched out wearily on
a tiny sunning-bank in the farthest corner of the Old Pasture, and had just about made up his mind that he would
go back that very night to the dear Old Briar-patch on the
Green Meadows, when a tiny rustle behind him made him
jump to his feet with his heart in his mouth. But instead
of the angry face of the old gray Rabbit he saw—what do
you think? Why, two of the softest, gentlest eyes peeping
at him from behind a big fern.

XI

Peter Rabbit Has a Sudden Change
of Mind

Whatever you decide to do
Make up your mind to see it through.
                                    Peter Rabbit

PETER RABBIT STARED at the two soft, gentle eyes peeping
at him from behind the big fern just back of the
sunning-bank in the far corner of the Old Pasture. He
had so fully expected to see the angry face of the big,
gray, old Rabbit who had made life so miserable for him
that for a minute he couldn't believe that he really saw
what he did see. And so he just stared and stared. It was
very rude. Of course it was. It was very rude indeed. It is
always rude to stare at any one. So it was no wonder that
after a minute the two soft, gentle eyes disappeared behind one of the great green leaves of the fern. Peter gave
a great sigh. Then he remembered how rude he had been
to stare so.

"I—I beg your pardon," said Peter in his politest manner, which is very polite indeed, for Peter can be very polite when he wants to be. "I beg your pardon. I didn't mean to frighten you. Please forgive me."

With the greatest eagerness Peter waited for a reply. You know it was because he had been so lonesome that he had left his home in the dear Old Briar-patch on the Green Meadows. And since he had been in the Old Pasture he had been almost as lonesome, for he had had no one to talk to. So now he waited eagerly for a reply. You see, he felt sure that the owner of such soft, gentle eyes must have a soft, gentle voice and a soft, gentle heart, and there was nothing in the world that Peter needed just then so much as sympathy. But though he waited and waited, there wasn't a sound from the big fern.

"Perhaps you don't know who I am. I'm Peter Rabbit, and I've come up here from the Green Meadows, and I'd like very much to be your friend," continued Peter after a while. Still there was no sound. Peter peeped from the corner of one eye at the place where he had seen the two soft, gentle eyes, but there was nothing to be seen but the gently waving leaf of the big fern. Peter didn't know just what to do. He wanted to hop over to the big fern and peep behind it, but he didn't dare to. He was afraid that whoever was hiding there would run away.

"I'm very lonesome; won't you speak to me?" said Peter, in his gentlest voice, and he sighed a deep, doleful sort of sigh. Still there was no reply. Peter had just about made up his mind that he would go over to the big fern when he saw those two soft, gentle eyes peeping from under a different leaf. It seemed to Peter that never in all his life had he seen such beautiful eyes. They looked so shy and bashful that Peter held his breath for fear that he would frighten them away.

After a time the eyes disappeared. Then Peter saw a little movement among the ferns, and he knew that whoever was there was stealing away. He wanted to follow, but something down inside him warned him that it was best to sit still. So Peter sat just where he was and kept perfectly still for the longest time. But the eyes didn't appear again, and at last he felt sure that whoever they belonged to had really gone away. Then he sighed another great sigh, for suddenly he felt more lonesome than ever. He hopped over to the big fern and looked behind it. There in the soft earth was a footprint, the footprint of a Rabbit, and it was *smaller* than his own. It seemed to Peter that it was the most wonderful little footprint he ever had seen.

"I believe," said Peter right out loud, "that I'll change my mind. I won't go back to the dear Old Briar-patch just yet, after all."

XII

Peter Learns Something from Tommy Tit

When you find a friend in trouble
Pass along a word of cheer.
Often it is very helpful
Just to feel a friend is near.
Peter Rabbit

"HELLO, PETER RABBIT! What are you doing way up here, and what are you looking so mournful about?"

Peter gave a great start of pleased surprise. That was the first friendly voice he had heard for days and days.

"Hello yourself, Tommy Tit!" shouted Peter joyously. "My, my, my, but I am glad to see you! But what are you doing up here in the Old Pasture yourself?"

Tommy Tit the Chickadee hung head down from the tip of a slender branch of a maple-tree and winked a saucy bright eye at Peter. "I've got a secret up here," he said.

Now there is nothing in the world Peter Rabbit loves more than a secret. But he cannot keep one to save him. No, Sir, Peter Rabbit can no more keep a secret than he can fly. He means to. His intentions are the very best in the world, but—

> Alas! alack! poor Peter's tongue
> Is very, very loosely hung.

And so, because he *must* talk and *will* talk every chance he gets, he cannot keep a secret. People who talk too much never can.

"What is your secret?" asked Peter eagerly.

Tommy Tit looked down at Peter, and his sharp little eyes twinkled. "It's a nest with six of the dearest little babies in the world in it," he replied.

"Oh, how lovely!" cried Peter. "Where is it, Tommy Tit?"

"In a hollow birch-stub," replied Tommy, his eyes twinkling more than ever.

"But where is the hollow birch-stub?" persisted Peter.

Tommy laughed. "That's my real secret," said he, "and if I should tell you it wouldn't be a secret at all. Now tell me what you are doing up here in the Old Pasture, Peter Rabbit."

Peter saw that it was of no use to tease Tommy Tit for his secret, so instead he poured out all his own troubles. He told how lonesome he had been in the dear Old Briar-patch on the Green Meadows because he didn't dare to

"Those eyes belong to little Miss Fuzzytail."

go about for fear of Old Man Coyote, and how at last he
had decided to visit the Old Pasture. He told how Hooty
the Owl had nearly caught him on his way, and then how,
ever since his arrival, he had been hunted by the big, gray,
old Rabbit so that he could neither eat nor sleep and had
become so miserable that at last he had made up his mind
to go back to the dear Old Briar-patch.

"Ho!" interrupted Tommy Tit, "I know him. He's Old Jed
Thumper, the oldest, biggest, crossest Rabbit anywhere
around. He's lived in the Old Pasture so long that he thinks
he owns it. It's a wonder that he hasn't killed you."

"I guess perhaps he would have only I can run faster
than he can," replied Peter, looking a little shame-faced
because he had to own up that he ran away instead of
fighting.

Tommy Tit laughed. "That's the very wisest thing you
could have done," said he. "But why don't you go back to
the dear Old Briar-patch on the Green Meadows?"

Peter hesitated and looked a wee bit foolish. Finally he
told Tommy Tit all about the two soft, gentle eyes he had
seen peeping at him from behind a big fern, and how he
wanted to know who the eyes belonged to.

"If that's all you want to know, I can tell you," said Tommy Tit, jumping out into the air to catch a foolish little
bug who tried to fly past. "Those eyes belong to little Miss
Fuzzytail, and she's the favorite daughter of Old Jed
Thumper. You take my advice, Peter Rabbit, and trot along
home to the Old Briar-patch before you get into any more
trouble. There's my wife calling. Yes, my dear, I'm coming! Chickadee-dee-dee!"

And with a wink and a nod to Peter Rabbit, off flew
Tommy Tit.

XIII

Little Miss Fuzzytail

*Foolish questions waste time, but wise
questions lead to knowledge.*

Peter Rabbit

"LITTLE MISS FUZZYTAIL!" Peter said it over and over again,
as he sat on the sunning-bank in the far corner of
the Old Pasture, where Tommy Tit the Chickadee had left
him.

"It's a pretty name," said Peter. "Yes, Sir, it's a pretty name.
It's the prettiest name I've ever heard. I wonder if she is
just as pretty. I—I—think she must be. Yes, I am quite
sure she must be." Peter was thinking of the soft, gentle
eyes he had seen peeping at him from behind the big fern,
and of the dainty little footprint he had found there afterward. So he sat on the sunning-bank, dreaming pleasant
dreams and wondering if he could find little Miss Fuzzytail if he should go look for her.

Now all the time, although Peter didn't know it, little
Miss Fuzzytail was very close by. She was right back in
her old hiding-place behind the big fern, shyly peeping
out at him from under a great leaf, where she was sure he
wouldn't see her. She saw the long tears in Peter's coat,
made by the cruel claws of Hooty the Owl, and she saw
the places where her father, Old Jed Thumper, had pulled
the hair out with his teeth. She saw how thin and miserable Peter looked, and tears of pity filled the soft, gentle
eyes of little Miss Fuzzytail, for, you see, she had a very
tender heart.

"He's got a very nice face," thought Miss Fuzzytail, "and he certainly was very polite, and I do love good manners. And Peter is such a nice sounding name! It sounds so honest and good and true. Poor fellow! Poor Peter Rabbit!" Here little Miss Fuzzytail wiped her eyes. "He looks so miserable I do wish I could do something for him. I—I—oh, dear, I do believe he is coming right over here! I guess I better be going. How he limps!"

Once more the tears filled her soft, gentle eyes as she stole away, making not the least little sound. When she was sure she was far enough away to hurry without attracting Peter's attention, she began to run.

"I saw him talking to my old friend Tommy Tit the Chickadee, and I just know that Tommy will tell me all about him," she thought, as she scampered along certain private little paths of her own.

Just as she expected, she found Tommy Tit and his anxious little wife, Phoebe, very busy hunting for food for six hungry little babies snugly hidden in a hollow near the top of the old birch-stub. Tommy was too busy to talk then, so little Miss Fuzzytail sat down under a friendly bramble-bush to rest and wait, and while she waited, she carefully washed her face and brushed her coat until it fairly shone. You see, not in all the Old Pasture, or the Green Forest, was there so slim and trim and neat and dainty a Rabbit as little Miss Fuzzytail, and she was very, very particular about her appearance.

By and by, Tommy Tit stopped to rest. He looked down at Miss Fuzzytail and winked a saucy black eye. Miss Fuzzytail winked back. Then both laughed, for they were very good friends, indeed.

"Tell me, Tommy Tit, all about Peter Rabbit," commanded little Miss Fuzzytail. And Tommy did.

XIV

Some One Fools Old Jed Thumper

You cannot judge a person's temper by his
size. There is more meanness in the head of
a Weasel than in the whole of a Bear.
Peter Rabbit

OLD JED THUMPER sat in his bull-briar castle in the middle of the Old Pasture, scowling fiercely and muttering to himself. He was very angry, was Old Jed Thumper. He was so angry that presently he stopped muttering and began to chew rapidly on nothing at all but his temper, which is a way angry Rabbits have.

The more he chewed his temper, the angrier he grew. He was big and stout and strong and gray. He had lived so long in the Old Pasture that he felt that it belonged to him and that no other Rabbit had any right there unless he said so. Yet here was a strange Rabbit who had had the impudence to come up from the Green Meadows and refused to be driven away. Such impudence!

Of course it was Peter Rabbit of whom Old Jed Thumper was thinking. It was two days since he had caught a glimpse of Peter, but he knew that Peter was still in the Old Pasture, for he had found fresh tracks each day. That very morning he had visited his favorite feeding ground, only to find Peter's tracks there. It had made him so angry that he had lost his appetite, and he had gone straight back to his bull-briar castle to think it over. At last Old Jed Thumper stopped chewing on his temper. He scowled more fiercely than ever and stamped the ground impatiently.

"I'll hunt that fellow till I kill him, or drive him so far from the Old Pasture that he'll never think of coming back. I certainly will!" he said aloud, and started forth to hunt.

Now it would have been better for the plans of Old Jed Thumper if he had kept them to himself instead of speaking aloud. Two dainty little ears heard what he said, and two soft, gentle eyes watched him leave the bull-briar castle. He started straight for the far corner of the Old Pasture where, although he didn't know it, Peter Rabbit had found a warm little sunning-bank. But he hadn't gone far when, from way off in the opposite direction, he heard a sound that made him stop short and prick up his long ears to listen. There it was again—thump, thump! He was just going to thump back an angry reply, when he thought better of it.

"If I do that," thought he, "I'll only warn him, and he'll run away, just as he has before."

So instead, he turned and hurried in the direction from which the thumps had come, taking the greatest care to make no noise. Every few jumps he would stop to listen. Twice more he heard those thumps, and each time new rage filled his heart, and for a minute or two he chewed his temper.

"He's down at my blueberry-patch," he muttered.

At last he reached the blueberry-patch. Very softly he crept to a place where he could see and not be seen. No one was there. No, Sir, no one was there! He waited and watched, and there wasn't a hair of Peter Rabbit to be seen. He was just getting ready to go look for Peter's tracks when he heard that thump, thump again. This time it came from his favorite clover-patch where he never allowed even his favorite daughter, little Miss Fuzzytail, to go. Anger nearly choked him as he hurried in that direction. But when he got there, just as before no one was to be seen.

So, all the morning long, Old Jed Thumper hurried from one place to another and never once caught sight of Peter Rabbit. Can you guess why? Well, the reason was that all the time Peter was stretched out on his warm sunning-bank getting the rest he so much needed. It was some one else who was fooling Old Jed Thumper.

XV

A Pleasant Surprise for Peter

Sticks will break and sticks will bend,
And all things bad will have an end.
Peter Rabbit

ALL MORNING, WHILE some one was fooling Old Jed Thumper, the cross old Rabbit who thought he owned the Old Pasture, Peter Rabbit lay stretched out on the warm little sunning-bank, dreaming of soft, gentle eyes and beautiful little footprints. It was a dangerous place to go to sleep, because at any time fierce Mr. Goshawk might have come that way, and if he had, and had found Peter Rabbit asleep, why, that would have been the end of Peter and all the stories about him.

Peter did go to sleep. You see, the sunning-bank was so warm and comfortable, and he was so tired and had had so little sleep for such a long time that, in spite of all he could do, he nodded and nodded and finally slipped off into dreamland.

Peter slept a long time, for no one came to disturb him. It was past noon when he opened his eyes and blinked up at jolly, round, red Mr. Sun. For a minute he couldn't remember where he was. When he did, he sprang to his feet and hastily looked this way and that way.

"My gracious!" exclaimed Peter. "My gracious, what a careless fellow I am! It's a wonder that Old Jed Thumper didn't find me asleep. My, but I'm hungry! Seems as if I hadn't had a good square meal for a year."

Peter stopped suddenly and began to wrinkle his nose. "Um-m!" said he, "if I didn't know better, I should say that there is a patch of sweet clover close by. Um-m, my, my! Am I really awake, or am I still dreaming? I certainly do smell sweet clover!"

Slowly Peter turned his head in the direction from which the delicious smell seemed to come. Then he whirled around and stared as hard as ever he could, his mouth gaping wide open in surprise. He blinked, rubbed his eyes, then blinked again. There could be no doubt of it; there on the edge of the sunning-bank was a neat little pile of tender, sweet clover. Yes, Sir, there it was!

Peter walked all around it, looking for all the world as if he couldn't believe that it was real. Finally he reached out and nibbled a leaf of it. It *was* real!

There was no doubt in Peter's mind then. Some one had put it there while Peter was asleep, and Peter knew that it was meant for him. Who could it have been?

Suddenly a thought popped into Peter's head. He stopped eating and hopped over to the big fern from behind which he had first seen the two soft, gentle eyes peeping at him the day before. There in the soft earth was a fresh footprint, and it looked very, very much like the footprint of dainty little Miss Fuzzytail!

Peter's heart gave a happy little jump. He felt sure now who had put the clover there. He looked wistfully about among the ferns, but she was nowhere to be seen. Finally, he hopped back to the pile of clover and ate it, every bit, and it seemed to him that it was the sweetest, tenderest clover he had ever tasted in all his life.

XVI

Peter Rabbit's Looking-glass

If people by their looks are judged,
  As judged they're sure to be,
Why each should always look his best,
  I'm sure you will agree.

Peter Rabbit

FOR THE FIRST time in his life Peter Rabbit had begun to think about his clothes. Always he had been such a happy-go-lucky fellow that it never had entered his head to care how he looked. He laughed at Sammy Jay for thinking so much of that beautiful blue-and-white coat he wears, and he poked fun at Reddy Fox for bragging so much about his handsome suit. As for himself, Peter didn't care how he looked. If his coat was whole, or in rags and tags, it was all the same to Peter.

But now Peter, sitting on the edge of his sunning-bank in the far corner of the Old Pasture, suddenly realized that he wanted to be good-looking. Yes, Sir, he wanted to be good-looking. He wished that he were bigger. He wished that he were the biggest and strongest Rabbit in the world. He wished that he had a handsome coat. And it was all because of the soft, gentle eyes of little Miss Fuzzytail that he had seen peeping out at him so often. He felt sure that it was little Miss Fuzzytail herself who had left the pile of sweet clover close by his sunning-bank the other day while he was asleep.

The fact is, Peter Rabbit was falling in love. Yes, Sir, Peter Rabbit was falling in love. All he had seen of little Miss Fuzzytail were her soft, gentle eyes, for she was very shy and had kept out of sight. But ever since he had first seen them, he had thought and dreamed of nothing else, until it seemed as if there were nothing in the world he wanted so much as to meet her. Perhaps he would have wanted this still more if he had known that it was she who had fooled her father, Old Jed Thumper, the big, gray, old Rabbit, so that Peter might have the long nap on the sunning-bank he so needed.

"I've just got to meet her. I've just got to!" said Peter to himself, and right then he began to wish that he were big and fine-looking.

"My, I must be a sight!" he thought. "I wonder how I do look, anyway. I must hunt up a looking-glass to find out."

Now when Peter Rabbit thinks of doing a thing, he wastes very little time. It was that way now. He started at once for the bit of swamp where he had first seen the tracks of Old Jed Thumper. He still limped from the wounds made by Hooty the Owl. But in spite of this he could travel pretty fast, and it didn't take him long to reach the swamp.

There, just as he expected, he found a looking-glass. What was it like? Why, it was just a tiny pool of water. Yes, Sir, it was a quiet pool of water that reflected the ferns growing around it and the branches of the trees hanging over it, and Peter Rabbit himself sitting on the edge of it. That was Peter's looking-glass.

For a long time he stared into it. At last he gave a great sigh. "My, but I am a sight!" he exclaimed.

He was. His coat was ragged and torn from the claws of Hooty the Owl and the teeth of Old Jed Thumper. The white patch on the seat of his trousers was stained and dirty from sitting down in the mud. There were burrs tangled in his waistcoat. He was thin and altogether a miserable looking Rabbit.

"It must be that Miss Fuzzytail just pities me. She certainly can't admire me," muttered Peter, as he pulled out the burrs.

For the next hour Peter was very busy. He washed and he brushed and he combed. When, at last, he had done all that he could, he took another look in his looking-glass, and what he saw was a very different looking Rabbit.

> "Though I am homely, lank and lean,
>   I can at least be neat and clean,"

said he, as he started back for the sunning-bank.

XVII

Peter Meets Miss Fuzzytail

> That this is true there's no denying—
> There's nothing in the world like trying.
> *Peter Rabbit*

PETER RABBIT WAS feeling better. Certainly he was looking better. You see, just as soon as Old Mother Nature saw that Peter was trying to look as well as he could, and was keeping himself as neat and tidy as he knew how, she was ready to help, as she always is. She did her best with the rents in his coat, made by the claws of Hooty the Owl and the teeth of Old Jed Thumper, and so it wasn't long before Peter's coat looked nearly as good as new. Then, too, Peter was getting enough to eat these days. Days and days had passed since he had seen Old Jed Thumper, and this had given him time to eat and sleep.

Peter wondered what had become of Old Jed Thumper. "Perhaps something has happened to him," thought Peter. "I—I almost hope something has." Then, being ashamed of such a wish, he added, "Something not very dreadful, but which will keep him from hunting me for a while and trying to drive me out of the Old Pasture."

Now all this time Peter had been trying to find little Miss Fuzzytail. He was already in love with her, although all he had seen of her were her two soft, gentle eyes, shyly peeping at him from behind a big fern. He had wandered here and sauntered there, looking for her, but although he found her footprints very often, she always managed to keep out of his sight. You see, she knew the Old Pasture so much better than he did, and all the little paths in it, that she had very little trouble in keeping out of his way. Then, too, she was very busy, for it was she who was keeping her cross father, Old Jed Thumper, away from Peter, because she was so sorry for Peter. But Peter didn't know this. If he had, I am afraid that he would have been more in love than ever.

The harder she was to find, the more Peter wanted to find her. He spent a great deal of time each day brushing his coat and making himself look as fine as he could, and while he was doing it, he kept wishing over and over again that something would happen so that he could show little Miss Fuzzytail what a smart, brave fellow he really was.

But one day followed another, and Peter seemed no nearer than ever to meeting little Miss Fuzzytail. He was thinking of this one morning and was really growing very down-hearted, as he sat under a friendly bramble-bush, when suddenly there was a sharp little scream of fright from behind a little juniper-tree.

Somehow Peter knew whose voice that was, although he never had heard it before. He sprang around the little juniper-tree and what he saw filled him with such rage that he didn't once stop to think of himself. There was little Miss Fuzzytail in the clutches of Black Pussy, Farmer Brown's cat, who often stole away from home to hunt in the Old Pasture. Like a flash Peter sprang over Black Pussy, and as he did so he kicked with all his might. The cat hadn't seen him coming, and the kick knocked her right into the prickly juniper-tree. Of course she lost her grip on little Miss Fuzzytail, who hadn't been hurt so much as frightened.

By the time the cat got out of the juniper-tree, Peter and Miss Fuzzytail were sitting side by side safe in the middle of a bull-briar patch.

"Oh, how brave you are!" sobbed little Miss Fuzzytail.

And this is the way that Peter Rabbit at last got his heart's desire.

XVIII

Tommy Tit Proves a Friend Indeed

> Nothing in all the world is so precious as a true friend.
>
> *Peter Rabbit*

AFTER PETER RABBIT had saved little Miss Fuzzytail from Black Pussy, the cat who belonged way down at Farmer Brown's house and had no business hunting in the Old Pasture, he went with her as near to her home as she would let him. She said that it wasn't necessary that he should go a single step, but Peter insisted that she needed him to see that no more harm came to her. Miss Fuzzytail laughed at that, for she felt quite able to take care of herself. It had been just stupid carelessness on her part that had given Black Pussy the chance to catch her, she said, and she was very sure that she never would be so careless again. What she didn't tell Peter was that she had been so busy peeping at him and admiring him that she had quite forgotten to watch out for danger for herself.

Finally she said that he could go part way with her. But when they were almost within sight of the bull-briar castle of her father, Old Jed Thumper, the big, gray Rabbit who thought he owned the Old Pasture, she made Peter turn back. You see, she was afraid of what Old Jed Thumper might do to Peter, and—well, the truth is she was afraid of what he might do to her if he should find out that she had made friends with Peter.

So Peter was forced to go back, but he took with him a half promise that she would meet him the next night up near his sunning-bank in the far corner of the Old Pasture.

After that there were many pleasant days for Peter Rabbit. Sometimes little Miss Fuzzytail would meet him, and sometimes she would shyly hide from him, but somehow, somewhere, he managed to see her every day, and so all the time in Peter's heart was a little song:

> "The sky is blue; the leaves are green;
>   The golden sunbeams peep between;
>   My heart is joyful as can be,
>   And all the world looks bright to me."

And then one day Old Jed Thumper found out all about how his daughter, little Miss Fuzzytail, and Peter Rabbit had become such good friends. Old Jed Thumper went into a terrible rage. He chewed and chewed with nothing in his mouth, that is, nothing but his temper, the way an angry Rabbit will. He vowed and declared that if he never ate another mouthful he would drive Peter Rabbit from the Old Pasture.

My, my, my, those were bad days for Peter Rabbit! Yes, Sir, those certainly were bad days! Old Jed Thumper had found out how little Miss Fuzzytail had been fooling him by making him think Peter was in parts of the Old Pasture in quite the opposite direction from where he really was. Worse still, he found Peter's favorite sunning-bank in the far corner of the Old Pasture and would hide near it and try to catch Peter every time Peter tried to get a few minutes' rest there. He did something worse than that.

One day he saw fierce Mr. Goshawk hunting. He let Mr. Goshawk almost catch him and then ducked under a bramble-bush. Then he showed himself again and once more escaped in the same way. So he led fierce Mr. Goshawk to a point where Mr. Goshawk could look down and see Peter Rabbit stretched out on his sunning-bank, trying to get a little rest. Right away Mr. Goshawk forgot all about Old Jed Thumper and sailed up in the sky from where he could swoop down on Peter, while Old Jed Thumper, chuckling to himself wickedly, hid where he could watch what would happen.

That certainly would have been the last of Peter Rabbit if it hadn't been for Tommy Tit the Chickadee. Tommy saw Mr. Goshawk and just in time warned Peter, and so Mr. Goshawk got only his claws full of soft earth for his pains, while Old Jed Thumper once more chewed on nothing in rage and disappointment. Dear me, dear me, those certainly were dreadful days for Peter Rabbit and little Miss Fuzzytail. You see, all the time little Miss Fuzzytail was terribly worried for fear Peter would be caught.

XIX

Old Man Coyote Pays a Debt

> Some little seeds of goodness
> You'll find in every heart,
> To sprout and keep on growing
> When once they get a start.
> *Peter Rabbit*

MATTERS WENT FROM bad to worse with Peter Rabbit and little Miss Fuzzytail. Peter would have made up his mind to go back to his old home in the dear Old Briarpatch on the Green Meadows, but he felt that he just couldn't leave little Miss Fuzzytail, and little Miss Fuzzytail couldn't make up her mind to go with Peter, because she felt that she just couldn't leave the Old Pasture, which always had been her home. So Peter spent his days and nights ready to jump and run from Jed Thumper, the gray old Rabbit who thought he owned the Old Pasture, and who had declared that he would drive Peter out.

Now Peter, as you know, had an old friend in the Old Pasture, Tommy Tit the Chickadee. One day Tommy took it into his head to fly down to the Green Meadows. There he found everybody wondering what had become of Peter Rabbit, for you remember Peter had stolen away from the dear Old Briar-patch in the night and had told no one where he was going. Now one of the first to ask Tommy Tit if he had seen Peter Rabbit was Old Man Coyote. Tommy told him where Peter was and of the dreadful time Peter was having. Old Man Coyote asked a lot of questions about the Old Pasture and thanked Tommy very politely as Tommy flew over to the Smiling Pool to call on Grandfather Frog and Jerry Muskrat.

That night Old Man Coyote started for the old pasture.

That night, after jolly, round, red Mr. Sun had gone to bed behind the Purple Hills, and the Black Shadows had crept over the Green Meadows, Old Man Coyote started for the Old Pasture. Now, he had never been there before, but he had asked so many questions of Tommy Tit, and he is so smart anyway, that it didn't take him long to go all through the Old Pasture and to find the bull-briar castle of Old Jed Thumper, who was making life so miserable for Peter Rabbit. He wasn't at home, but Old Man Coyote's wonderful nose soon found his tracks, and he followed them swiftly, without making a sound. Pretty soon he came to a bramble-bush, and under it he could see Old Jed Thumper.

For just a minute he chuckled, a noiseless chuckle, to himself. Then he opened his mouth and out came that terrible sound which had so frightened all the little people on the Green Meadows when Old Man Coyote had first come there to live.

"Ha, ha, ha! Ho, ho, ho! Hee, hee, hee! Ha, ho, hee, ho!"

Old Jed Thumper never had heard anything like that before. It frightened him so that before he thought what he was doing he had jumped out from under the bramble-bush. Of course this was just what Old Man Coyote wanted. In a flash he was after him, and then began such a race as the Old Pasture never had seen before. Round and round, this way and that way, along the cow paths raced Old Jed Thumper with Old Man Coyote at his heels, until at last, out of breath, so tired that it seemed to him he couldn't run another step, frightened almost out of his senses, Old Jed Thumper reached his bull-briar castle and was safe.

Then Old Man Coyote laughed his terrible laugh once more and trotted over to the tumble-down stone-wall in which his keen nose told him Peter Rabbit was hiding.

"One good turn deserves another, and I always pay my debts, Peter Rabbit," said he. "You did me a good turn some time ago down on the Green Meadows, when you told me how Granny and Reddy Fox were planning to make trouble for me by leading Bowser the Hound to the place where I took my daily nap, and now we are even. I don't think that old gray Rabbit will dare to poke so much as his nose out of his bull-briar castle for a week. Now I am going back to the Green Meadows. Good night, Peter Rabbit, and don't forget that I always pay my debts."

"Good night, and thank you, Mr. Coyote," said Peter, and then, when Old Man Coyote had gone, he added to himself in a shame-faced way: "I didn't believe him when he said that he guessed we would be friends."

XX

Little Miss Fuzzytail Whispers "Yes"

Love is a beautiful, wonderful thing.
　　There's nothing quite like it on all the
　　　　green earth.
'Tis love in the heart teaches birdies to sing,
　　And gives the wide world all its joy and
　　　　its mirth.

Peter Rabbit

PETER RABBIT WAS finding this out. Always he had been happy, for happiness had been born in him. But the happiness he had known before was nothing to the happiness that was his when he found that he loved little Miss Fuzzytail and that little Miss Fuzzytail loved him.

Peter was sure that she did love him, although she wouldn't say so. But love doesn't need words, and Peter had seen it shining in the two soft, gentle eyes of little Miss Fuzzytail. So Peter was happy in spite of the trouble that Old Jed Thumper, the big, gray Rabbit who was the father of little Miss Fuzzytail, had made for him in the Old Pasture.

He had tried very hard, very hard indeed, to get little Miss Fuzzytail to go back with him to the dear Old Briar-patch on the Green Meadows, but in spite of all he could say she couldn't make up her mind to leave the Old Pasture, which, you know, had been her home ever since she was born. And Peter couldn't make up his mind to go back there and leave her, because—why, because he loved her so much that he felt that he could never, never be happy without her. Then, when Old Jed Thumper was hunting Peter so hard that he hardly had a chance to eat or sleep, had come Old Man Coyote the Wolf and given Old Jed Thumper such a fright that for a week he didn't dare poke so much as his nose out of his bull-briar castle.

Now, although Old Man Coyote didn't know it, his terrible voice had frightened little Miss Fuzzytail almost as much as it had Old Jed Thumper. You see, she never had heard it before. She didn't even know what it was, and all that night she had crouched in her most secret hiding-place, shivering and shaking with fright. The next morning Peter had found her there. She hadn't slept a wink, and she was still too frightened to even go look for her breakfast.

"Oh, Peter Rabbit, did you hear that terrible noise last night?" she cried.

"What noise?" asked Peter, just as if he didn't know anything about it.

"Why, that terrible voice!" cried little Miss Fuzzytail, and shivered at the thought of it.

"What was it like?" asked Peter.

"Oh, I can't tell you," said little Miss Fuzzytail. "It wasn't like anything I ever had heard before. It was something like the voice of Hooty the Owl and the voice of Dippy the Loon and the voice of a little yelping dog all in one, and it was just terrible!"

"Oh," replied Peter, "you must mean the voice of my friend, Old Man Coyote. He came up here last night just to do me a good turn because I once did him a good turn."

Then he told all about how Old Man Coyote had come to the Green Meadows to live, and how he was smarter than even old Granny Fox, but he didn't tell her how he himself had once been frightened almost out of a year's growth by that terrible voice, or that it was because he hadn't really believed that Old Man Coyote was his friend that had led him to leave the Old Briar-patch and come up to the Old Pasture.

"Is—is he fond of Rabbits?" asked little Miss Fuzzytail.

Peter was quite sure that he was.

"And do you think he'll come up here hunting again?" she asked.

Peter didn't know, but he suspected that he would.

"Oh, dear," wailed little Miss Fuzzytail. "Now, I never, never will feel safe again!"

Then Peter had a happy thought. "I tell you what," said he, "the safest place in the world for you and me is my dear Old Briar-patch. Won't you go there now?"

Little Miss Fuzzytail sighed and dropped a tear or two. Then she nestled up close to Peter. "Yes," she whispered.

XXI

Peter and Little Miss Fuzzytail
Leave the Old Pasture

A danger past is a danger past,
   So why not just forget it?
Watch out instead for the one ahead
   Until you've safely met it.

Peter Rabbit

As soon as little Miss Fuzzytail had agreed to go with him to make her home in the dear Old Briar-patch down on the Green Meadows, Peter Rabbit fairly boiled over with impatience to start. He had had so much trouble in the Old Pasture that he was afraid if they waited too long little Miss Fuzzytail might change her mind, and if she should do that—well, Peter didn't know what he would do.

But Peter, who always had been so happy-go-lucky, with no one to think about but himself, now felt for the first time re-sponsi-bil-ity. That's a big word, but it is a word that everybody has to learn the meaning of sometime. Johnny Chuck learned it when he made a home for Polly Chuck in Farmer Brown's orchard, and tried to keep it a secret, so that no harm would come to Polly. It means taking care of other people or other people's things, and feeling that you must take even greater care than you would of yourself or your own things. So, while Peter himself would have been willing to take chances, and might even have made the journey down to the dear Old Briar-patch in broad daylight, he felt that that wouldn't do at all for little Miss Fuzzytail; that he must avoid every possible chance of danger for her.

So Peter waited for a dark night, not too dark, you know, but a night when there was no moon to make great patches of light, but only the kindly little Stars looking down and twinkling in the friendly way they have. At last there was just such a night. All the afternoon little Miss Fuzzytail went about in the Old Pasture saying good-by to her friends and visiting each one of her favorite little paths and hiding-places, and I suspect that in each one she dropped a tear or two, for you see she felt sure that she never would see them again, although Peter had promised that he would bring her back to the Old Pasture for a visit whenever she wanted to come.

At last it was time to start. Peter led the way. Very big and brave and strong and important he felt, and very timid and frightened felt little Miss Fuzzytail, hopping after him close at his heels. You see, she felt that she was going out into the Great World, of which she knew nothing at all.

"Oh, Peter," she whispered, "supposing we should meet Reddy Fox! I wouldn't know where to run or hide."

"We are not going to meet Reddy Fox," replied Peter, "but if we should, all you have to do is to just keep your eyes on the white patch on the seat of my trousers and follow me. I have fooled Reddy so many times that I'm not afraid of him."

Never in all his life had Peter been so watchful and careful. That was because he felt his re-sponsi-bil-ity. Every few jumps he would stop to sit up and look and listen. Then little Miss Fuzzytail would nestle up close to him, and Peter's heart would swell with happiness, and he would feel, oh, so proud and important. Once they heard the sharp bark of Reddy Fox, but it was a long way off, and Peter smiled, for he knew that Reddy was hunting on the edge of the Green Forest.

Once a dim shadow swept across the meadow grass ahead of them. Peter dropped flat in the grass and kept perfectly still, and little Miss Fuzzytail did just as he did, as she had promised she would.

"Wha— what was it?" she whispered.

"I think it was Hooty the Owl," Peter whispered back, "but he didn't see us." After what seemed like a long, long time they heard Hooty's fierce hunting call, but it came from way back of them on the edge of the Old Pasture. Peter hopped to his feet.

"Come on," said he. "There's nothing to fear from him now."

So slowly and watchfully Peter led the way down across the Green Meadows while the little Stars looked down and twinkled in the most friendly way, and just as jolly, round, red Mr. Sun started to kick off his bedclothes behind the Purple Hills they reached the dear Old Briar-patch.

"Here we are!" cried Peter.

"Oh, I'm so glad!" cried little Miss Fuzzytail, hopping along one of Peter's private little paths.

XXII

Sammy Jay Becomes Curious

Learn all you can about others, but keep
your own affairs to yourself.
                                    Peter Rabbit

OF COURSE IT was Sammy Jay who first found out that Peter Rabbit was back in the dear Old Briar-patch. Sammy took it into his head to fly over there the very morning of Peter's home-coming. Indeed, little Miss Fuzzy-tail hadn't had time to half see the dear Old Briar-patch which, you know, was to be her new home, when Peter saw Sammy Jay coming. Now Peter was not quite ready to have all the world know that there was a Mrs. Peter, for of course that was what little Miss Fuzzytail was now that she had come to make her home with Peter. They wanted to keep by themselves for a little while and just be happy with each other. So as soon as Peter saw Sammy Jay headed towards the Old Briar-patch, he hid little Miss Fuzzytail under the thickest sweet-briar bush, and then hurried out to the nearest sweet-clover patch.

Of course Sammy Jay saw him right away, and of course Sammy was very much surprised.

"Hello, Peter Rabbit! Where'd you come from?" he shouted, as he settled himself comfortably in a little poplar-tree growing on the edge of the Old Briar-patch.

"Oh," said Peter with a very grand air, "I've been on a long journey to see the Great World."

"Which means," said Sammy Jay with a chuckle, "that you've been in the Old Pasture all this time, and let me tell you, Peter Rabbit, the Old Pasture is a very small part of the Great World. By the way, Tommy Tit the Chickadee was down here the other day and told us all about you. He said that you had fallen in love with little Miss Fuzzytail, and he guessed that you were going to make your home up there. What's the matter? Did her father, Old Jed Thumper, drive you out?"

"No, he didn't!" snapped Peter angrily. "It's none of your business what I came home for, Sammy Jay, but I'll tell you just the same. I came home because I wanted to."

Sammy chuckled, for he dearly loves to tease Peter and make him angry. Then the imp of mischief, who seems always to live just under that smart cap of Sammy's, prompted him to ask: "Did you come home alone?"

Now Peter couldn't say "yes" for that would be an untruth, and whatever faults Peter may have, he is at least truthful. So he just pretended not to have heard Sammy's question.

Now when Sammy had asked the question he had thought nothing about it. It had just popped into his head by way of something to say. But Sammy Jay is sharp, and he noticed right away that Peter didn't answer but began to talk about other things.

"Ha, ha!" thought Sammy to himself, "I believe he didn't come alone. I wonder now if he brought Miss Fuzzytail with him."

Right away Sammy began to peer down into the Old Briar-patch, twisting and turning so that he could see in every direction, and all the time talking as fast as his tongue could go. Two or three times he flew out over the Old Briar-patch, pretending to try to catch moths, but really so that he could look down into certain hiding-places. The last time that he did this he spied little Mrs. Peter, who was, you know, Miss Fuzzytail. At once Sammy Jay started for the Green Forest, screaming at the top of his voice:

"Peter Rabbit's married! Peter Rabbit's married!"

XXIII

Peter Introduces Mrs. Peter

It's what you do for others,
    Not what they do for you,
That makes you feel so happy
    All through and through and through.
                    Peter Rabbit

PETER RABBIT MADE a very wry face as he listened to Sammy Jay shrieking at the top of his voice as he flew through the Green Forest and over the Green Meadows,

"Peter Rabbit's married! Peter Rabbit's married!" He saw the Merry Little Breezes who, you know, are the children of Old Mother West Wind, start for the dear Old Briar-patch as soon as they heard Sammy Jay, and he knew that they would be only the first of a lot of visitors. He hurried to where Mrs. Peter was hiding under a sweet-briar bush.

"Do you hear what that mischief-maker, Sammy Jay, is screaming?" asked Peter.

Mrs. Peter nodded. "Don't—don't you think it sounds kind of—well, kind of *nice*, Peter?" she asked in a bashful sort of way.

Peter chuckled. "It sounds more than *kind* of nice to me," said he. "Do you know, I used to think that Sammy Jay never did and never could say anything nice, but I've just changed my mind. Though he isn't saying it to be nice, it really is the nicest thing I've ever heard him say. We haven't been able to keep our secret, so I think the very best thing we can do is to invite everybody to call. Then we can get it over with and have a little time to ourselves. Here come the Merry Little Breezes, and I know that they will be glad to take the invitations for us."

Mrs. Peter agreed, for she thought that anything Peter did or suggested was just about right. So the Merry Little Breezes were soon skipping and dancing over the Green Meadows and through the Green Forest with this message:

"Mr. and Mrs. Peter Rabbit will be at home in the Old Briar-patch to their friends to-morrow afternoon at shadow-time."

"Why did you make it at shadow-time?" asked Mrs. Peter.

"Because that will give all our friends a chance to come," replied Peter. "Those who sleep through the day will have waked up, and those who sleep through the night will not have gone to bed. Besides, it will be safer for some of the

smallest of them if the Black Shadows are about for them
to hide in on their way here."

"How thoughtful you are," said little Mrs. Peter with a
little sigh of happiness.

Of course, every one who could walk, creep, or fly
headed for the Old Briar-patch the next day at shadow-
time, for almost every one knows and loves Peter Rabbit,
and of course every one was very anxious to meet Mrs.
Peter. From the Smiling Pool came Billy Mink, Little Joe
Otter, Jerry Muskrat, Spotty the Turtle, and old Grand-
father Frog. From the Green Forest came Bobby Coon,
Unc' Billy Possum and Mrs. Possum, Prickly Porky the
Porcupine, Whitefoot the Woodmouse, Happy Jack the
Gray Squirrel, Chatterer the Red Squirrel, Blacky the Crow,
Sammy Jay, Ol' Mistah Buzzard, Mistah Mockingbird, and
Stickytoes the Treetoad. From the Green Meadows came
Danny Meadow Mouse, Old Mr. Toad, Digger the Badger,
Jimmy Skunk, and Striped Chipmunk, who lives near the
old stone-wall between the edge of the Green Meadows
and the Green Forest. Johnny and Polly Chuck came down
from the Old Orchard and Drummer the Woodpecker
came from the same place.

Of course Old Man Coyote paid his respects, and when
he came everybody but Prickly Porky and Digger the
Badger and Jimmy Skunk made way for him with great
respect. Granny and Reddy Fox and Hooty the Owl didn't
call, but they sat where they could look on and make fun.
You see, Peter had fooled all three so many times that they
felt none too friendly.

Very proud looked Peter as he stood under a bramble-
bush with Mrs. Peter by his side and introduced her to his
many friends, and very sweet and modest and retiring
looked little Mrs. Peter as she sat beside him. Everybody
said that she was "too sweet for anything," and when Reddy
Fox overheard that remark he grinned and said:

"Not for me!   She can't be too sweet for me, and I hope
I'll have a chance to find out just how sweet she is."

What do you suppose he meant?

XXIV

Danny Meadow Mouse Warns
Peter Rabbit

Good advice is always needed
But, alas! is seldom heeded.
                    Peter Rabbit

DANNY MEADOW MOUSE waited until all the rest of Peter
Rabbit's friends had left the Old Briar-patch after pay-
ing their respects to Peter and Mrs. Peter. He waited for
two reasons, did Danny Meadow Mouse. In the first place,
he had seen old Granny Fox and Reddy Fox hanging about
a little way off, and though they had disappeared after a
while, Danny had an idea that they were not far away, but
were hiding so that they might catch him on his way home.
Of course, he hadn't the slightest intention of giving them
the chance. He had made up his mind to ask Peter if he
might spend the night in a corner of the Old Briar-patch,
and he was very sure that Peter would say he might, for he
and Peter are very good friends, very good friends indeed.

The second good reason Danny had for waiting was
this very friendship. You see, Peter had been away from
the Green Meadows so long that Danny felt sure he
couldn't know all about how things were there now, and
so he wanted to warn Peter that the Green Meadows were

not nearly as safe as before Old Man Coyote had come there to live. So Danny waited, and when all the rest of the callers had left he called Peter to one side where little Mrs. Peter couldn't hear. Danny stood up on his hind legs so as to whisper in one of Peter's ears.

"Do you know that Old Man Coyote is the most dangerous enemy we have, Peter Rabbit? Do you know that?" he asked.

Peter Rabbit shook his head. "I don't believe that, Danny," said he. "His terrible voice has frightened you so that you just think him as bad as he sounds. Why, Old Man Coyote is a friend of mine."

Then he told Danny how Old Man Coyote had done him a good turn in the Old Pasture in return for a good turn Peter had once done him, and how he said that he always paid his debts.

Danny Meadow Mouse looked doubtful. "What else did he say?" he demanded. "Nothing, excepting that we were even now," replied Peter.

"Ha!" said Danny Meadow Mouse.

The way he said it made Peter turn to look at him sharply.

"Ha!" said Danny again. "If you are even, why you don't owe him anything, and he doesn't owe you anything. Watch out, Peter Rabbit! Watch out! I would stick pretty close to the Old Briar-patch with Mrs. Peter if I were you. I would indeed. You used to think old Granny Fox pretty smart, but Old Man Coyote is smarter. Yes, Sir, he is smarter! And every one of the rest of us has got to be smarter than ever before to keep out of his clutches. Watch out, Peter Rabbit, if you and Old Man Coyote are even. Now, if you don't mind, I'll curl up in my old hiding-place for the night. I really don't dare go back home to-night."

Of course Peter told Danny Meadow Mouse that he was welcome to spend the night in the Old Briar-patch, and thanked Danny for his warning as he bade him good-night. But Peter never carries his troubles with him for long, and by the time he had rejoined little Mrs. Peter he was very much inclined to laugh at Danny's fear.

"What did that funny little Meadow Mouse have to say?" asked Mrs. Peter.

Peter told her and then added, "But I don't believe we have anything to fear from Old Man Coyote. You know he is my friend."

"But I don't know that he is mine!" replied little Mrs. Peter, and the way she said it made Peter look at her anxiously. "I believe Danny Meadow Mouse is right," she continued. "Oh, Peter, you will watch out, won't you?"

And Peter promised her that he would.

XXV

Peter Rabbit's Heedlessness

Heedlessness is just the twin of thoughtless-
    ness, you know,
And where you find them both at once, there
    trouble's sure to grow.
                                Peter Rabbit

PETER RABBIT DIDN'T mean to be heedless. No, indeed! Oh, my, no! Peter thought so much of Mrs. Peter, he meant to be so thoughtful that she never would have a thing to worry about. But Peter was heedless. He always was heedless. This is the worst of a bad habit—you can try to let go of it, but it won't let go of you. So it was with Peter. He had been heedless so long that now he actually didn't know when he was heedless.

When there was nobody but himself to think about, and no one to worry about him, his heedlessness didn't so much matter. If anything had happened to him then, there would have been no one to suffer. But now all this was changed. You see, there was little Mrs. Peter. At first Peter had been perfectly content to stay with her in the dear Old Briar-patch. He had led her through all his private little paths, and they had planned where they would make two or three more. He had showed her all his secret hiding-places and the shortest way to the sweet-clover patch. He had pointed out where the Lone Little Path came down to the edge of the Green Forest and so out on to the Green Meadows. He had shown her where the Crooked Little Path came down the hill. Little Mrs. Peter had been delighted with everything, and not once had she complained of being homesick for the Old Pasture.

But after a little while Peter began to get uneasy. You see in the days before Old Man Coyote had come to live on the Green Meadows, Peter had come and gone about as he pleased. Of course he had had to watch out for Granny and Reddy Fox, but he had had to watch out for them ever since he was a baby, so he didn't fear them very much in spite of their smartness. He felt quite as smart as they and perhaps a little bit smarter. Anyway, they never had caught him, and he didn't believe they ever would. So he had come and gone as he pleased, and poked his nose into everybody's business, and gossiped with everybody.

Of course it was quite natural that Peter should want to call on all his old friends and visit the Green Forest, the Old Orchard, the Laughing Brook, and the Smiling Pool. Probably Mrs. Peter wouldn't have worried very much if it hadn't been for the warning left by Danny Meadow Mouse. Danny had said that Old Man Coyote was more to be feared than all the Hawk family and all the Fox family together, because he was smarter and slyer than any of them. At first Peter had looked very serious, but after Danny had gone back to his own home Peter had laughed at Danny for being so afraid, and he began to go farther and farther away from the safe Old Briar-patch.

One day he had ventured as far as halfway up the Crooked Little Path. He was thinking so hard of a surprise he was planning for little Mrs. Peter that he forgot to watch out and almost ran into Old Man Coyote before he saw him. There was a hungry look, such a hungry look in Old Man Coyote's eyes as he grinned and said "Good morning" that Peter didn't even stop to be polite. He remembered that Jimmy Skunk's old house was near, and he reached it just one jump ahead of Old Man Coyote.

"I thought you said that we were friends," panted Peter, as he heard Mr. Coyote sniffing at the doorway.

"So we were until I had paid my debt to you. Now that I've paid that, we are even, and it is everybody watch out for himself," replied Old Man Coyote. "But don't forget that I always pay my debts, Peter Rabbit."

XXVI

Peter Rabbit Listens to Mrs. Peter

Safety first is a wise rule for those who would live long.

Peter Rabbit

Peter Rabbit was glad enough to get back to the dear Old Briar-patch after his narrow escape from Old Man Coyote by dodging into Jimmy Skunk's old house halfway up the hill. And little Mrs. Peter was glad enough to have him, you may be sure. She had been watching Peter when he so heedlessly almost ran into Old Man Coyote, and it had seemed to her as if her heart stopped beating until Peter reached the safety of that old house of Jimmy Skunk just one jump ahead. Then she saw Old Man Coyote hide in the grass near by and she was terribly, terribly afraid that Peter would be heedless again and come out, thinking that Mr. Coyote had gone.

Poor little Mrs. Peter! She was so anxious that she couldn't sit still. She felt that she just had to do something to warn Peter. She stole out from the dear Old Briarpatch and halfway to where Old Man Coyote was hiding. He was so busy watching the doorway of the old house where Peter was hiding that he didn't notice her at all. Little Mrs. Peter found a bunch of tall grass behind which she could sit up and still not be seen. So there she sat without moving for a long, long time, never once taking her eyes from Old Man Coyote and the doorway of the old house. By and by she saw Peter poke his nose out to see if the way was clear. Old Man Coyote saw him too, and began to grin. It was a hungry, wicked-looking grin, and it made little Mrs. Peter very, very angry indeed.

She waited just a minute longer to make sure that Peter was where he could see her, and then she thumped the ground very hard, which, you know, is the way Rabbits signal to each other. Peter heard it right away and thumped back that he would stay right where he was, though right down in his heart Peter thought that little Mrs. Peter was just nervous and foolish, for he was sure that Old Man Coyote had given up and gone away long ago.

Now of course Old Man Coyote heard those thumps, and he knew just what they meant. He knew that he never, never could catch Peter so long as Mrs. Peter was watching him and ready to warn Peter. So he came out of his

"Oh, you dear stupid!" replied little Mrs. Peter.

hiding-place with an ugly snarl and sprang toward little Mrs. Peter just to frighten her. He laughed as he watched her run and, all breathless, dive into the dear, safe Old Briar-patch, and then he trotted away to his favorite napping-place.

As soon as Peter was sure that he was safe he started for home, and there little Mrs. Peter scolded him soundly for being so heedless and thoughtless.

Peter didn't have a word to say. For a long time he sat thinking and thinking, every once in a while scratching his head as if puzzled. Little Mrs. Peter noticed it.

"What's the matter with you, Peter?" she asked finally.

"I'm just studying what Old Man Coyote means by telling me one day that he is my friend, and proving it by doing me a good turn, and then trying to catch me the very next time he sees me. I don't understand it," said Peter, shaking his head.

"Oh, you dear old stupid!" replied little Mrs. Peter. "Now, you listen to me. You did Old Man Coyote a good turn and he paid you back by doing you a good turn. That made you even, didn't it?"

Peter nodded.

"Well, then you are right back where you started from, and Old Man Coyote doesn't see any reason why he should treat you any differently than at first, and I don't see why he should either, when I come to think it over. I tell you what, Peter, the thing for you to do is to keep doing good turns to Old Man Coyote so that he will always be in debt to you. Then he will always be your friend."

As little Mrs. Peter stopped speaking, Peter sprang to his feet. "The very thing! he cried. "It's sort of a Golden Rule, and I do believe it will work."

"Of course it will," replied little Mrs. Peter.

XXVII

Mistah Mocker Plays a Joke on Mrs. Peter

This little point remember, please—
There's little gained by those who tease.
Peter Rabbit

MISTAH MOCKER THE Mockingbird had been very late in coming up to the Green Meadows from way down South. The truth is, he had almost decided not to come. You see, he loves the sunny southland so much, and all who live there love him so much, that if it hadn't been for Unc' Billy Possum and Ol' Mistah Buzzard he never, never would have thought of leaving, even for a little while. Unc' Billy and Ol' Mistah Buzzard are particular friends of his, very particular friends, and he felt that he just had to come up for a little visit.

Now Mistah Mocker reached the Green Meadows just after Peter Rabbit had brought little Mrs. Peter down from the Old Pasture to live with him in the dear Old Briar-patch. He knew that little Mrs. Peter didn't know anything about him, for he never had visited the Old Pasture where she had spent her life. But he knew all the bird people who do live there, for he had met them in the sunny southland, where they spent the winter.

"I believe I'll go pay my respects to Mrs. Peter," said Mistah Mocker one day, winking at Ol' Mistah Buzzard. Ol' Mistah Buzzard chuckled and winked back.

"Ah cert'nly hopes yo' all will behave yo'self right proper and not forget that yo' is a member of one of the oldest families in the Souf," said he.

Mistah Mocker looked quite solemn as he promised to behave himself, but there was a twinkle in his eyes as he flew towards the Old Briar-patch. There he hid in a thick tangle of vines. Now it happened that Peter Rabbit had gone over to the sweet-clover patch, and little Mrs. Peter was quite alone. Somehow she got to thinking of her old home, and for the first time she began to feel just a wee, wee bit homesick. It was just then that she heard a familiar voice. Little Mrs. Peter pricked up her ears and smiled happily.

"That's the voice of Tommy Tit the Chickadee, and it must be that his wife is with him, for I hear him calling 'Phoebe! Phoebe!' How lovely of them to come down to see me so soon."

Just then she heard another voice, a deep, beautiful, ringing voice, a voice that she loved. It was the voice of Veery the Thrush. "Oh!" cried little Mrs. Peter, and then held her breath so as not to miss one note of the beautiful song. Hardly had the song ended when she heard the familiar voice of Redeye the Vireo. Little Mrs. Peter clapped her hands happily. "It must be a surprise party by my old friends and neighbors of the Old Pasture!" she cried. "How good of them to come way down here, and how glad I shall be to see them!"

With that little Mrs. Peter hurried over to the tangle of vines from which all the voices seemed to come and eagerly peered this way and that way for a sight of her friends. But all she saw was a stranger wearing a very sober-colored suit. He was very polite and told her that he was an old friend of Peter Rabbit.

"If you are a friend of Peter, then you are a friend of mine," said little Mrs. Peter very prettily. "Have you seen anybody in this tangle of vines since you arrived? I am sure some friends of mine are here, but I haven't been able to find them."

"No," said the stranger, who was, of course, Mistah Mocker the Mockingbird. "I haven't seen any one here, and I don't think there has been any one here but myself."

"Oh, yes, indeed there has!" cried little Mrs. Peter. "I heard their voices, and I couldn't possibly be mistaken in those, especially the beautiful voice of Veery the Thrush. I—I would like very much to find them."

Mistah Mocker had the grace to look ashamed of himself when he saw how disappointed little Mrs. Peter was. Very softly he began to sing the song of Veery the Thrush.

Little Mrs. Peter looked up quickly. "There it is!" she cried. "There—" she stopped with her mouth gaping wide open. She suddenly realized that it was Mistah Mocker who was singing.

"I—I'm very sorry," he stammered. "I did it just for a joke and not to make you feel bad. Will you forgive me?"

"Yes," replied little Mrs. Peter, "if you will come here often at shadow-time and sing to me." And Mistah Mocker promised that he would.

XXVIII

News from the Old Briar-patch

To use your eyes is very wise
And much to be commended;
But never see what cannot be
For such as you intended.

Peter Rabbit

JENNY WREN IS a busybody. Yes, Sir, she certainly is a busybody. If there is anything going on in her neighborhood that she doesn't know about, it isn't because she doesn't try to find out. She is so small and spry that it is hard work to keep track of her, and she pops out at the most unexpected times and places. Then, before you can say a word, she is gone.

And in all the Old Orchard or on the Green Meadows there is not to be found another tongue so busy as that of Jenny Wren. It is sharp sometimes, but when she wants it to be so there is none smoother. You see she is a great gossip, is Jenny Wren, a great gossip. But if you get on the right side of Jenny Wren and ask her to keep a secret, she'll do it. No one knows how to keep a secret better than she does.

How it happened nobody knows, but it did happen that when Peter Rabbit came home to the dear Old Briar-patch, bringing Mrs. Peter with him, Jenny Wren didn't hear about it. Probably it was because the new home which she had just completed was so carefully hidden that the messengers sent by Peter to invite all his friends to call didn't find it, and afterward she was so busy with household affairs that she didn't have time to gossip. Anyway, Peter had been back some time before Jenny Wren knew it. She was quite upset to think that she was the last to hear the news, but she consoled herself with the thought that she had been attending strictly to her duties, and now that her children were able to look out for themselves she could make up for lost time.

Just as soon as she could get away, she started for the Old Briar-patch. She wanted to hear all about Peter's adventures in the Old Pasture and to meet Mrs. Peter. But like a great many other busybodies, she wanted to find out all she could about Peter's affairs, and she thought that the surest way to do it was not to let Peter know that she was about until she had had a chance to use her sharp little eyes all she wanted to. So when she reached the Old

Briar-patch, she didn't make a sound. It didn't take her long to find Peter. He was sitting under one of his favorite bramble-bushes smiling to himself. He smiled and smiled until Jenny Wren had to bite her tongue to keep from asking what was pleasing him so.

"He looks tickled almost to death over something, but very likely if I should ask him what it is he wouldn't tell me," thought Jenny Wren. "I guess I'll look around a bit first. I wonder where Mrs. Peter is."

So leaving Peter to smile to his heart's content, she went peeking and peering through the Old Briar-patch. Of course it wasn't a nice thing to do, not a bit nice. But Jenny Wren didn't stop to think of that. By and by she saw something that made her flutter all over with excitement. She looked and looked until she could sit still no longer. Then she hurried back to where Peter was sitting. He was still smiling.

"Oh, Peter Rabbit, it's perfectly lovely!" she cried.

Peter looked up quickly, and a worried look chased the smile away. "Hello, Jenny Wren! Where did you come from? I haven't seen you since I got back," said he.

"I've been so busy that I haven't had time to call before," replied Jenny. "I know what you've been smiling about, Peter, and it's perfectly splendid. Has everybody heard the news?"

"No," said Peter, "nobody knows it but you, and I don't want anybody else to know it just yet. Will you keep it a secret, Jenny Wren?"

Now Jenny was just bursting with desire to spread the news, but Peter looked so anxious that finally she promised that she would keep it to herself, and she really meant to. But though Peter looked greatly relieved as he watched her start for home, he didn't smile as he had before. "I wish her tongue didn't wag so much," said he.

XXIX

Jimmy Skunk Visits Peter Rabbit

It's hard to keep a secret when you fairly ache
    to tell;
So not to know such secrets is often quite as
    well.

Peter Rabbit

ON HER WAY home from the Old Briar-patch, Jenny Wren
stopped to rest in a bush beside the Crooked Little
Path that comes down the hill, when who should come
along but Jimmy Skunk. Now just as usual Jenny Wren
was fidgeting and fussing about, and Jimmy Skunk grinned as he watched her.

"Hello, Jenny Wren!" said he. "What are you doing
here?"

"I'm resting on my way home from the Old Briar-patch,
if you must know, Jimmy Skunk!" replied Jenny Wren,
changing her position half a dozen times while she was
speaking.

"Ho, ho, ho!" laughed Jimmy Skunk. "Do you call that
resting! That's a joke, Jenny Wren. Resting! Why, you
couldn't sit still and rest if you tried!"

"I could so! I'm resting right now, so there, Jimmy
Skunk!" protested Jenny Wren in a very indignant tone of
voice, and hopped all over the little bush while she was
speaking. "I guess if you knew what I know, you'd be excited too."

"Well, I guess the quickest way for me to know is for
you to tell me," replied Jimmy. "I'm just aching to be excited."

"The quickest way for me to know is for you to tell me,"
replied Jimmy.

Jimmy grinned, for you know Jimmy Skunk never does get excited and never hurries, no matter what happens.

"You'll have to keep right on aching then," replied Jenny Wren, with a saucy flirt of her funny little tail. "There's great news in the Old Briar-patch, and I'm the only one that knows it, but I've promised not to tell."

Jimmy pricked up his ears. "News in the Old Briar-patch must have something to do with Peter Rabbit," said he. "What has Peter done now?"

"I'll never tell! I'll never tell!" cried Jenny Wren, growing so excited that it seemed to Jimmy as if there was danger that she would turn herself inside out. "I promised not to and I never will!" Then, for fear that she would in spite of herself, she flew on her way home.

Jimmy watched her out of sight with a puzzled frown. "If I didn't know that she gets so terribly excited over nothing, I'd think that there really is some news in the Old Briar-patch," he muttered to himself. "Anyway, I haven't anything better to do, so I believe I'll drop around that way and make Peter Rabbit a call."

He found Peter in some sweet clover just outside the Old Briar-patch, and it struck Jimmy that Peter looked uncommonly happy. He said as much.

"I am," replied Peter, before he thought. Then he added hastily, "You see, I've been uncommonly happy ever since I returned with Mrs. Peter from the Old Pasture."

"But I hear there's great news over here in the Old Briar-patch," persisted Jimmy Skunk. "What is it, Peter?"

Peter pretended to be very much surprised. "Great news!" he repeated. "Great news! Why, what news can there be over here? Who told you that?"

"A little bird told me," replied Jimmy slyly.

"It must have been Jenny Wren!" said Peter, once more speaking before he thought.

"Then there *is* news over here!" cried Jimmy triumphantly. "What is it, Peter?"

But Peter shook his head as if he hadn't the slightest idea and couldn't imagine. Jimmy coaxed and teased, but all in vain. Finally he started for home no wiser than before.

"Just the same, I believe that Jenny Wren told the truth and that there *is* news over in the Old Briar-patch," he muttered to himself. "Something has happened over there, and Peter won't tell. I wonder what it can be."

XXX

Reddy Fox Learns the Secret

Nothing that you ever do,
    Nothing good or nothing bad,
But has effect on other folks—
    Gives them pain or makes them glad.
                            Peter Rabbit

OF COURSE JENNY Wren didn't mean to tell the secret of the old Briar-patch, because she had promised Peter Rabbit that she wouldn't. But she didn't see any harm in telling every one she met that there was a secret there, at least that there was great news there, and so, because Jenny Wren is a great gossip, it wasn't long before all the little people on the Green Meadows and in the Green Forest and around the Smiling Pool had heard it and were wondering what the news could be.

After Jimmy Skunk's visit came a whole string of visitors to the Old Briar-patch. One would hardly have left before another would appear. Each one tried to act as if he had just happened around that way and didn't want to pass Peter's home without making a call, but each one asked so many questions that Peter knew what had really brought him there was the desire to find out what the news in the Old Briar-patch could be. But Peter was too smart for them, and they all went away no wiser than they came, that is, all but one, and that one was Reddy Fox.

There isn't much going on in the Green Forest or on the Green Meadows that Reddy doesn't know about. He is sly, is Reddy Fox, and his eyes are sharp and his ears are keen, so little happens that he doesn't see or hear about. Of course he heard the foolish gossip of Jenny Wren and he pricked up his ears.

"So there's news down in the Old Briar-patch, is there? A secret that Jenny Wren won't tell? I think I'll trot down there and make Peter a call. Of course he'll be glad to see me."

Reddy grinned wickedly as he said this to himself, for he knew that there was no one for whom Peter Rabbit had less love, unless it was old Granny Fox.

So Reddy trotted down to the Old Briar-patch. Peter saw him coming and scowled, for he guessed right away what Reddy was coming for, and he made ready to an-swer all Reddy's questions and still tell him nothing, as he had with all the others who had called.

But Reddy asked no questions. He didn't once men-tion the fact that he had heard there was news in the Old Briar-patch. He didn't once speak of Jenny Wren. He just talked about the weather and the Old Pasture, where Peter had made such a long visit, and all the time was as pleas-ant and polite as if he and Peter were the dearest of friends.

But while he was talking, Reddy was using those sharp eyes and those keen ears of his the best he knew how.

But the Old Briar-patch was very thick, and he could see only a little way into it, and out of it came no sound to hint of a secret there. Then Reddy began to walk around the Old Briar-patch in quite the most matter-of-fact way, but as he walked that wonderful nose of his was testing every little breath of air that came out of the Old Briar-patch. At last he reached a certain place where a little stronger breath of air tickled his nose. He stopped for a few minutes, and slowly a smile grew and grew. Then, without saying a word, he turned and trotted back towards the Green Forest.

Peter Rabbit watched him go. Then he joined Mrs. Peter in the heart of the Old Briar-patch. "My dear," he said, with a sigh that was almost a sob, "Reddy Fox has found out our secret."

"Never mind," said little Mrs. Peter brightly. "It would have to be found out soon, anyway."

Trotting back up the Lone Little Path, Reddy Fox was grinning broadly. "It *is* news!" said he. "Jenny Wren was right, it *is* news! But I don't believe anybody else knows it yet, and I hope they won't find it out right away, least of all Old Man Coyote. What a wonderful thing a good nose is! It tells me what my eyes cannot see nor my ears hear."

XXXI

Blacky the Crow Has Sharp Eyes

> Mischief always waits to greet
> Idle hands and idle feet.
>
> *Peter Rabbit*

THAT IS WHAT a lot of people say about Blacky the Crow. Of course it is true that Blacky does get into a lot of mischief, but if people really knew him they would find that he isn't as black as he looks. In fact, Blacky the Crow does a whole lot of good in his own peculiar way, but people are always looking for him to do bad things, and you know you most always see what you expect to see. Thus the good Blacky does isn't seen, while the bad is, and so he has grown to have a reputation blacker than the coat he wears.

But this doesn't worry Blacky the Crow. No, Sir, it doesn't worry him a bit. You see he has grown used to it. And then he is so smart that he is never afraid of being caught when he does do wrong things. No one has sharper eyes than Blacky, and no one knows better how to use them. There is very little going on in the Green Forest or on the Green Meadows that he misses when he is about.

The day after Reddy Fox visited the Old Briar-patch and with his wonderful nose found out Peter Rabbit's secret, Blacky just happened to fly over the Old Briar-patch on his way to Farmer Brown's cornfield. Now, being over the Old Briar-patch, he could look right down into it and see all through it. Just as he reached it, he remembered having heard Sammy Jay say something about gossipy little

Jenny Wren's having said that there was great news there. He hadn't thought much about it at the time, but now that he was right there, he might as well have a look for himself and see if there was any truth in it.

So Blacky the Crow flew a little lower, and his sharp eyes looked this way and that way through all the bramble-bushes of the Old Briar-patch. He saw Peter Rabbit right away and winked at him. He thought Peter looked worried and anxious.

"Peter must have something on his mind," thought Blacky. "I wonder where Mrs. Peter is."

Just then he caught sight of her under the thickest growing sweet-briar bush. He had opened his mouth to shout, "Hello, Mrs. Peter," when he saw something that surprised him so that he didn't speak at all. He almost forgot to flap his wings to keep himself in the air. He hovered right where he was for a few minutes, looking down through the brambles. Then with a hoarse chuckle, he started for the Smiling Pool, forgetting all about Farmer Brown's cornfield. "Caw, caw, caw!" he shrieked, "Peter Rabbit's got a family! Peter Rabbit's got a family!"

Reddy Fox heard him and ground his teeth. "Now Old Man Coyote will know and will try to catch those young Rabbits, when they ought to be mine because I found out about them first," he grumbled.

Jimmy Skunk heard Blacky and grinned broadly. "So that's the great news Jenny Wren found out!" said he. "I hope Peter will take better care of his babies than he ever has of himself. I must call at once."

Redtail the Hawk heard, and he smiled too, but it wasn't a kindly smile like Jimmy Skunk's. "I think young Rabbit will taste very good for a change," said he.

XXXII

Peter Rabbit's Nursery

With home, the home you call your own,
It really doesn't matter where,
There is no place, in all the world,
That ever will or can compare.
                                    Peter Rabbit

THE NEWS WAS out at last, thanks to Blacky the Crow.
Peter Rabbit had a family! Yes, Sir, Peter Rabbit had a
family! Right away the Old Briar-patch became the most
interesting place on the Green Meadows to all the little
people who live there and in the near-by Green Forest. Of
course all of Peter's friends called as soon as ever they
could. They found Peter looking very proud, and very
important, and very happy. Mrs. Peter looked just as proud,
and just as happy, but she also looked very anxious. You
see, while she was very glad to have so many friends call,
there were also other visitors. That is, they were not ex-
actly callers, but they hung around the outside of the Old
Briar-patch, and they seemed quite as much interested as
the friends who really called. Indeed, they seemed more
interested.

Who were they? Why, Reddy Fox was one. Then there
was Old Man Coyote, also Redtail the Hawk and Digger
the Badger, and just at dusk Hooty the Owl. They all
seemed very much interested indeed, but every time little
Mrs. Peter saw them, she shivered. You see, she couldn't
help thinking that there was a dreadful hungry look in
their eyes, and if the truth is to be told, there probably
was.

But happy-go-lucky Peter Rabbit didn't let this worry him. Hadn't he grown up from a teeny-weeny baby and been smart enough to escape all these dangers which worried Mrs. Peter so? And if he could do it, of course his own babies could do it, with him to teach them and show them how. Besides, they were too little to go outside of the Old Briar-patch now. Indeed, they were too little to go outside their nursery, which was in a clump of sweet-briar bushes in the very middle of the Old Briar-patch, and Peter felt that they were perfectly safe.

"It isn't time to worry yet," said Peter to little Mrs. Peter, as he saw the fright in her eyes as the shadow of Redtail passed over them. "I don't believe in borrowing trouble. Time enough to worry when there is something to worry about, and that won't be until these little scallawags of ours are big enough to run around and get into mischief. Did you ever see such beautiful babies in all your life?"

For a minute the worried look left little Mrs. Peter, and she gazed at the four little helpless babies fondly. "No," she replied softly, "I never did. Oh, Peter, they are perfectly lovely! This one is the perfect image of you, and I'm going to call him Little Pete. And don't you think his brother looks like his grandfather? I think we'll call him Little Jed."

Peter coughed behind his hand as if something had stuck in his throat. He had no love for Little Jed's grandfather, Old Jed Thumper, the big, gray, old Rabbit who had tried so hard to drive him from the Old Pasture, but he didn't say anything. If Mrs. Peter wanted to name this one Little Jed, he wouldn't say a word. Aloud he said:

"I think, my dear, that this one looks just as you must have looked when you were little, and so we'll call her Fuzzy. And her sister we'll call Wuzzy," continued Peter. "Was ever there such a splendid nursery for baby Rabbits?"

"I don't believe there ever was, Peter. It's better than my old nursery in the Old Pasture," replied little Mrs. Peter, as with a sigh of perfect happiness she stretched out beside their four babies.

And Peter softly tiptoed away to the nearest sweet-clover patch with his heart almost bursting with pride.

Of the doings of Peter and Mrs. Peter Rabbit and their four children there are many more stories, so many that one book will not hold all of them. Besides, Bowser the Hound insists that I must write a book about him, and I have promised to do it right away. So the next book will be Bowser the Hound. *

THE END.